ADVANCE REVIEWS

"This fast paced political thriller offers a much needed fresh and multidimensional examination of student unrest on both sides of the Pacific. By switching points-of-view, Kuo shows a literary craftsman at work and proves once again that fiction counts."
— Ishmael Reed, writer and media critic, *Barack Obama and the Jim Crow Media: The Return of the Nigger Breakers*

"This is a story about the parallel histories of the Three Gorges Dam in China and the Grand Coulee Dam in the U.S., a meditation on the emergence of truth from improbable fiction, and a literary illustration of playful seriousness. Alex Kuo is a one-of-a-kind writer whose works recall the finest moments in Thomas Pynchon, Michael Ondaatje, and Karen Tei Yamashita."
— Wen Jin, scholar and literary critic, *Bridging the Chasm: An Asian American Critique of U.S. and Chinese Multiculturalisms*

"Alex Kuo's brilliant and original *The Man Who Dammed the Yangtze* tells a parallel tale for our time. Global corporations and their politician minions have come to rule. Two startled, compassionate mathematicians—one American, the other Chinese—foresee the disasters that compulsive dam-building will trigger. Alex Kuo's ocean-swimming, epic poem of a novel, co-locates and pinpoints the back-story to future crisis our planet can still be spared."
— Al Young, poet and writer, actor and musician, *Something about the Blues*

PREVIOUS REVIEWS

"Kuo writes with one of the most unique intelligences and imaginations in English language literature."
— Robert Abel, review in *Willow Springs*

"Alex Kuo is a mainstay of Chinese-American and Asian-American writing. He has helped to create this field by producing

some of its most important works and by defining the field. His concerns are large and universal—the ecological landscape of the American West, politics, history, and, of course, human emotions. As a citizen of many cultures, he has taken on the responsibility of integrating his prodigious knowledge of many peoples."
> — Maxine Hong Kingston, writer, *The Woman Warrior*,
> *Tripmaster Monkey, I Love a Broad Margin to My Life*

"In his impressive body of work spanning 40 years, Alex Kuo consistently pushes the limits of literary genres while defying some of society's most deeply entrenched assumptions. It is easy to see the influence his voice has had not only on writers but also on our collective views of race, culture, and politics. The smallest details have the power to burrow far into the imagination. There is the Tiananmen dissident, now safe in the U.S., who contemplates which Revlon lipstick color will best convey 'young, energetic and dedicated to democracy' to the media; the woman in worn-torn 1940s Chongqing, China, who once commanded 'the best upstairs table in the Ritz where everyone kowtowed to her' but who is now reduced to living in caves and foraging for food; and the quiet Oshkosh, Wisconsin, mathematics professor who ultimately breaks under yet another torrent of racist epithets. In fusing the political and the literary, Mr. Kuo illuminates over and over again the profound power of art."
> — Pauline Chen, *New York Times* medical columnist,
> *Final Examination: A Surgeon's Reflections on Mortality*

"Because he can pack multiple ideas into the smallest of spaces, reading Alex Kuo is best done twice. Once for beauty and again for meaning."
> — Richard Wallace, review in *Seattle Times*

"No one writes like this—no one else can. Kuo does it the hard way, with an uncommon artistry. Read this and you'll never see China in the same light again."
> — Xu Xi, writer, *Habit of a Foreign Sky*

The Man Who Dammed the Yangtze

ALEX KUO

Haven
BOOKS

ACKNOWLEDGMENTS

Thanks to the editors of *Hunger Mountain*, *Mascara* and *Three Coyotes* in which earlier versions of "Crossing Algoma," "Crossing Stalin Boulevard," "The Meeting," "The Tea Shop," "Howard Johnson's," "Last Class" and "Bridge" first appeared.

THE MAN WHO DAMMED THE YANGTZE

Published in Hong Kong by Haven Books Ltd
www.havenbooksonline.com

ISBN 978-988-19195-6-4

This book is for Stephen.

It is also for G and Ge, whose lives of courage and stamina have been remembered and sustained by their beloved with astonishment and admiration. I hope this novel's reshaping of their moments got their stories right. That is the point of fiction, isn't it.

OTHER BOOKS BY ALEX KUO

The Window Tree

New Letters from Hiroshima and Other Poems

Changing the River

Chinese Opera

Lipstick and Other Stories

This Fierce Geography

Panda Diaries

White Jade and Other Stories

A Chinaman's Chance

CONTENTS

PART ONE

PART TWO

PART THREE

Part One

(1968)

Oshkosh

1. CROSSING ALGOMA

His parents did not name him *G*. In fact, his parents did not read German, but in honor of the neurotic Franz Kafka whose work they had read in English, and to assimilate into what they saw as the burgeoning trans-national and trans-cultural 20th century, they named him *Gregor S*, diaspora or not. When he could not explain his name *Gregor* to his third-grade teacher, he accepted her shortened version, *G*, a one-syllable name more negotiable for his dream position in the baseball infield, shortstop, much in the same way his parents' Chinese names were anglicized by the INS at Angel Island. So twenty-some years later, this same G is waiting for the traffic to clear before crossing Algoma Boulevard in his jeans, ironed white shirt and shades to teach his Tuesday 7:30 differential-equations class in the new Clow classroom building, on the campus of this Midwestern state university.

This is his second teaching job in as many years, having left South Dakota in shock, fright, and eventually, rebellion. It was there a year ago he had realized his sheltered background—a boys' prep school in Connecticut, and then MIT—had not prepared him for the nasty turns of life. No one had whispered to him, *Watch out for the dilemma, the big one* that tents over every ambiguity, contradiction and betrayal—not his parents, intent on a stable and secure life for him, nor his third-grade teacher who, with the best of intentions, had been his biggest booster. This dilemma hadn't even surfaced as an independent choice assignment in an advanced probability and statistics class in college where he had majored in mathematics.

Last year, this university's basketball team made it to the quarterfinals of the NIT, and its twirling Silver Twins' only falter in the finals of the National Baton Queen competition kept them from the trophy. In a big-time Minneapolis radio interview later, the Silver Twins had commented that it had been their moment in history, their 15 seconds in the sun, and that they were on their way to a reception at the governor's mansion in Pierre, home of Congressional Medal of Honor recipient and United States Marine Corps F4F Wildcat fighter ace who'd shot down 26 Mitsubishi Zeroes, Governor Joe Foss, who would later become the first American Football League Commissioner. What the hell more do you want from life, G? Ain't two players on the NIT alternate All-American squad enough? Ain't their appearances on the *Ed Sullivan* and *Lawrence Welk Shows* enough? What's the matter with you boy? What makes you think another school in another state would be any different?

Besides, South Dakotans don't participate in daylight savings time because they don't want to meddle with God's time. So on an early, early spring morning, G had found himself among the lesser 11.11% in the state's population, next to the Sioux under house arrest. The only fucking chink in the entire state, and he had to be hobbled between the Santees and the Rosebuds. The final wreath was laid when the Dean of Women, Virginia V. Vordsdorff, led all the virgin gals on campus in a Maypole celebration, singing and dancing around the Campanile, the tallest, all-state prick in the flattened cornfields east of the Oahe Dam, border to border. Amen, amen, amen.

Just as G is about to cross Algoma, he feels a slight tug on the graded homework he's carrying to class. It's Joyce, easily his best student, always first with the answers, always correct, although that consistency is beginning to irritate G. He suspects that she has learned to manipulate the calculations with shortcuts, and just this morning in the shower he had thought about challenging her on it. For now, she has a question for him, this freshman from South Beloit who's not even a math major but is taking this class just for fun.

"Let's talk on the other side," he manages to say while throwing away his cigarette, shifting his papers to his right side and removing his shades.

"We had a meeting last night," Joyce smiles.

"Who's we?"

"Oh, sorry, the BSU, I mean the Black Student Union. With last year's recruitment, there're more than 130 of us now."

Point-zero-one-eight-five-seven-one-four registers with G, about 1.86% of the 7,000 total student enrollment, or about one fifth of one percent of the town's population.

"We need a faculty advisor to be officially recognized as a student organization, and we want you."

Cute, real cute, like Joyce is.

"You gotta be kidding, me?"

"Well, you're the closest to being colored. We thought that ..." Looking into her professor's deep-brown eyes, Joyce left the sentence unfinished.

"I know, I know, there's no black on the faculty. But what about Chang, he's senior, tenured, and chair of poli sci?"

"He doesn't count," she smiles again, a real cupcake this time.

G already knows this Dr. David Chang, or knows all he wants to know about this dude, the only other non-white person on the faculty. Chang's not a chink, but a regular social scientist, so he claimed. Social scientists' objectivity cannot be compromised by taking positions on the war, Chang had argued when asked to join a teach-in and present a lecture on his specialization, 20th-century Southeast Asian politics. The bastard stays away from all the major issues in life, remaining neutral in order to be accepted, suffocating himself in his yearning to be loved, then loved and tenured as nothing.

"Please slow down, you're always moving so fast." Then, catching up with G and crooking her head, she adds, "We need you."

"No you don't, just as you don't need differential equations—DE is just time consuming busy work, like whittling. You just need someone to sign for you and get into trouble for it, don't you? We're going to be late for class."

Some students on their way to Clow slow down and appear disturbed, staring at them standing maybe just a little bit too close, as their conversation certainly doesn't appear to be about an exponential function substitution or the test next week. What is it that is making them stop and stare, a) black and non-black, b) student and professor, c) girl and boy, d) two of the above, or e) none of the above?

Joyce pretends these students don't exist, and G, not as used to it, looks in their direction pissed off and defiant, mentally noting the most arrogant ones, a couple of them in his DE class, hah, hah.

"Listen Joyce, we've got this class now. Let's talk at the noon rally, okay?"

"Where you going to be?"

"You know where I'm going to be," G smiles at her and holds the door open.

Changchun

2. CROSSING STALIN BOULEVARD

Halfway around the world in the same semester, Ge is crossing Stalin Boulevard, heading toward campus for an emergency teaching staff meeting. When the department political leader who's never in the office for more than a few minutes a day (*oh, he's at the post office, or, oh, he's getting more paper for the duplicating machine, or, oh, he's at the Public Security Bureau*, or, most of the time, *oh, he's at a meeting*) came by her apartment last evening to inform her about this political session, she could tell from his teeth-baring smile that something very nasty was brewing. Having seen his kind and that look and that tone of voice before, she is not nervous about this meeting; from her past, she knows that there will be life after all, after men like that.

Having barely finished her final class in finite numbers and successfully defended her dissertation at Qinghua University in May, only moments ahead of the fomenting Red Guards, she just wanted to get as far away from them as possible. The ultimate teenage revenge drama was beginning to unfold in Beijing—a morality play anonymously staged and controlled by party ventriloquists in which two decades of sacrifice, repression, anger, fear, intimidation and frustration was given the opportunity to throw off all restraint. Raw, unfettered energy, stingers looking for victims. And China's never been short of scapegoats, each generation offering up its own social enemies. Some ten years older and knowing better, Ge wanted no part of the crazy schemes buzzing around the Qinghua undergraduate talk-heads who were about to go out of control.

Posters had started appearing everywhere. *Vigilance against the feudal elements. Down with old customs, old habits, old culture and old thinking.* Some argued that those meaningless, bourgeois requirements for a mathematics degree were the remnants of Soviet, or worse, American hegemonic influences, and they wanted their degrees in one year, MDs in two. With his personal impotent ax to grind, Mao Tse-tung had given them his nod of approval, and the movement took off. Her dissertation director, Professor Luo, had told her the Red Guards were never really in charge of anything but the theatrical mayhem, although their actions claimed many, many innocent bystanders — the real beneficiaries of their drama were the political cadres who silently manipulated the teenagers' actions for their own career advancement. Her classmates were beginning to repeat stories of beatings and public humiliations — teachers, librarians, the elderly, parents, performers of Peking operas, even the metonymical mailmen who only delivered the news.

When the stories turned to whispers, Ge knew she wanted out. With the firm support of Professor Luo, who met her at Qinghua's south gate with her unsigned diploma because no administrator dared to come to campus let alone hold graduation exercises, she was able to catch a train for the northeast. There with Professor Luo's strong letter of recommendation, she found a teaching job in Jilin Province three months later.

So for a year Ge had taught some basic courses — beginning and advanced calculus, advanced algebra, and an unusual seminar on the language of numbers. But then students had started missing her classes last spring and didn't turn in homework at all. Some had not even shown up for their final exam. At this key university well known for its mathematics department, truancy just didn't happen, and Ge had started to wonder if the Cultural Revolution, like summer, had just taken a long time finding its way here to Changchun, north of North Korea.

A cold breeze is blowing in the middle of this October and Ge's already wearing a sweater. Even the tails on the Long March overcoat on Mao's statue at the north end of the boulevard are whipping in the wind, but in the wrong direction. At seven degrees, it must be at least 10 degrees colder here than she'd grown used to going to school in Beijing, and at least 15 colder than Suzhou where she was raised. The heating and cooking smoke and soot from low-grade coal is turning everything in Changchun grey, the sidewalks, trees, buildings, the tongue and the sky and dreams, all grey, grey and more grey, the grey of the Soviet MiG-15s at the airport.

She takes a shortcut past the hospital, but a crowd of students is beginning to gather. Paying more attention, she sees that they are younger than her students. They are more like those gathered at the gates to Qinghua University a year ago, those she had ran away from. A few of them are wearing red armbands, and a girl no older than fifteen is in the front. She has carefully tucked her braids under her red cap and, despite her baggy uniform of blue trousers and white shirt, she is wearing brand new white sandals. She has buckled a heavy brown belt around her middle.

"Pigtails," she says, "pigtails are a residue of feudalism."

The gathering echoes approval.

"Pigtails make washing and weaving and arranging time-consuming," she continues.

Even with her short, Beijing-bobbed hair that she touches to make sure, Ge is beginning to get uncomfortable. She has witnessed this scene before.

"Taking care of pigtails wastes time, time better spent doing manual labor. And the soap and shampoo needed for its maintenance is a wanton waste of the nation's wealth." And pointing to the doors of the hospital behind her, she adds, "It's not even sanitary."

At this last statement, the crowd cheers, and she throws off her cap, unveiling her long braids. Someone in the front hands her a pair of grade-school scissors. She tilts her head and lets her braids fall forward, which she gathers together with her free hand and begins ceremonially to cut above the rubber bands holding them together in one, no, two, no, three snips. Then she flings

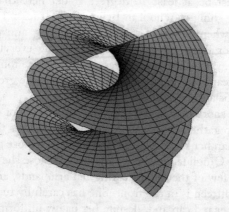

the two braids into the air high above the crowd, and as they sail up end over end, they form the embedded surfaces of a pair of perfect, independent and twirling finite topological helicoids, $2 \times \{f[a,b](u,v) = (a \times v \times \cos(u), a \times v \times \sin(u), b \times u)\}$, where $0 \leq u \leq 2 \times \pi$, $-d < v < d$ $d > 0$.

Even before these teenagers have time to respond with their thunderous applause, Ge has already crossed the street in the other direction, pulling her bag closer to her body and buttoning the lapels on her coat, hiding a shoulder shudder under its collar.

3. THE TRI-DELTS

It's noon in front of Dempsey. There must be at least 100 students and faculty gathered here in front of the barricade, not bad considering the administration had put a ban on demonstrations on university property. But there isn't the usual agitation, one or two voices ringing out, little murmurs of dissent. Instead there's an overwhelming silence as if everyone's holding a collective breath. G looks for Joyce, and then to the front where he's beginning to see little spots of flashing light.

They seem to be coming from the direction of several carefully dressed girls facing the crowd. They are cordoned together safely by Oshkosh PD officers and Winnebago County sheriff deputies who have pretty much stayed in the background with the undercover federal officers in the last two years, a period of campus demonstrations supporting civil rights and railing against the war in Vietnam.

G stops a friend and asks, "Hey, what's this?"

Before he can answer, Joyce's at G's side.

"You probably don't want to know, but they're Tri-Delt sisters taking Polaroid pictures."

Just before their weekly chapter meeting last night, Joyce continues, these sisters had heard President Richard Nixon call campus protesters the "scum of the earth" on the evening news, the NBC peacock spraying its umbrella of colors. So these patriotic Delta Delta Delta sisters had decided to do something voluntarily for their country. They knew some officers in uniform, as well as in plainclothes, had been around campus and the residencies, looking for help in identifying the student leaders and faculty participating in these demonstrations, teach-ins and sit-ins. Now they were doing their thing: taking pictures of these scum, identifying whom they could and jotting their names on the backs, and turning them in to the proper authorities.

"You're kidding me, no?"

"What do you think?"

This is the Tri-Delt's retaliation against the North Vietnamese Tet Offensive launched just eight months ago (welcome to the presidency, Dickie Nixon); it is their parallel to Mayor Richard Daley's "It's not going to happen in my city" said only a month ago at the National Democratic Presidential Convention at the Hilton in Chicago; and it is their body-count variation on the Raven Program, Operation Ranch Hand and the Phoenix Program all rolled into one. The combinations are staggering. And G notes that some of these sisters come from Appleton, Wisconsin, a leisurely fifteen-minute drive along the Winnebago lakeshore from here, home of Joseph McCarthy, the Godzilla in the United States' Asian foreign policy since the end of WWII. Our public schools have done their job. Give me your tired, your poor, your huddled masses and they will wear the American flag as their shoulder patch forever.

"Joyce, how do you know all this shit?"

This is nothing, she says, after some 300 years of keeping the ear to the ground for survival. "I see and hear what should get into the media, but doesn't."

The crowd is beginning to disperse, and the sisters walk into Old Main in the company of Ray "Rocket" Ramsden, who's smiling for the first time since becoming the university's vice president.

G turns to Joyce who's looking at him for an answer.

"I owe you one. You're taking DE when you don't need it. If I just did what I needed to, I wouldn't even be at this non-demonstration. I've got to say yes; I'll be BSU's advisor."

"Hah, hah, I knew you would. Thanks. And you don't have to come to any meetings."

"You mean all I have to do is sign?"

"That's easier than having to remake the sign," Joyce says, walking away.

G looks after her in the beautiful October Wisconsin sunlight, wondering if he's missed some shortcut in the logic of her remark, determined he's going to work it out himself by transforming it into a linear Diophantine equation, hoping there won't be a congruency problem in the remainder.

4. THE MEETING

Inside the auditorium, Ge avoids sitting with her male colleagues in the mathematics department who are gathered near the back and are suddenly quiet at the sight of her. Instead she finds her friend Tang Li sitting alone two rows up. A teacher of foreign languages and literature, she is also in exile from the south, although she keeps her hair shoulder-length and usually parted on both sides.

"Did you see those teenagers in front of the gate to the Geology University," Tang Li asks, agitated. "Just frightful troglodytes who need spanking. They should be taken home for a cup of warm goat milk, unsweetened."

She doesn't like teenagers, and had said to Ge just last week they should be locked up with each other until they are fit for life. It's also the reason she and her husband don't have any children, even though they have been married for over ten years. But it's moot, even if they had any. Their parents are gone. One at the hands of the Japanese in Nanjing and the other to the Kuomintang during Mao's Long March north, so they couldn't pawn any offspring off on them during the teenage years, as so many of today's parents are doing.

"No, I came the other way, but they are also at the hospital. I'd seen them in Beijing two years ago, but I thought this was too far north for them."

"You don't know Changchun, Ge. After you're here long enough, you'll learn that every kind eventually comes here and uses it for a doormat."

Tang Li then begins an inventory: the Hans, Manchus, Mongols, Muslims, Zunghars, white Russians, Soviets, Koreans, even the Germans, Dutch and the Americans too, but probably the worst were the Japanese and their factories of death, the biochemical experimental camps of the Imperial Japanese Army's Units 100, 565, and 731 between 1932 and 1945.

"Eventually you'll recognize them, those hyphenated ones, Korean-Chinese, Russian-Chinese, and worse, the Japanese-Chinese, those that have not suicided or been dropped by their parents at birth, either sex. Given the ugliness of people, they're not seen that much in public, but hide out in neighborhoods here and there, embarrassed and unforgiven."

A man Ge recognizes only as the University's vice president walks to the front with a stack of papers, a doctrinal speech that has been Xeroxed and is being passed out. Tang Li hands Ge a copy, and she looks at the title: *Down with Feudalism and the Dust of Foreign Hegemony Now — Why the People Must be the Broom that Sweeps out Chairman Mao's Enemies — Be Good Soldiers in the Wind that Marches Forward or Die a Glorious Death.* She looks down at the title again, between the lines, between the words, within the words, once, twice, three times, but Ge still doesn't understand it.

"My, my, my," Tang Li nudges her, clucking. "This title's like a triple Japanese haiku, and it functions the same as the concluding couplet of a Shakespearean sonnet, like it was written by a committee." She then raises her eyebrows. "This is written in October Changchun all right, with the prevailing wind and dust blowing here from the Soviets to the north, and what remains of Japanese culture that the Soviets did not loot after China was auctioned off at the Yalta Conference."

"This is like many of the Beijing speeches and political struggle-sessions I've been through."

"Yes, I've heard. Incredible! This is a country of realists, at least most of the time, and here our leaders are trying to seduce us with slogans, metaphors and homilies. Teach us with allegories? Such bozos!"

"Shhhhh," Ge whispers, pressing a finger to her lips and looking back at her male colleagues who are staring at her and Tang Li.

The PA system clicks on, and the vice president begins the meeting by reading the text that has just been passed out verbatim. Thirty minutes later he sets down the speech and begins his personal admonitions. Most of the faculty members are either dozing or are busy reading newspapers, grading assignments or writing letters, especially those sitting in the back behind the math department contingency. Most of the party members are in the front rows busy keeping vigilance, taking facsimile notes and occasionally turning around to see who isn't paying attention.

"We must pay attention to what this speech says here," the vice president emphasizes by putting his fist down on its text, creating a loud, crackling electrical feedback in the sound system. "Outside this campus, teenagers are beginning to gather, as some of you have noticed. It is just a matter of time before they will come here too. My duty is to keep this university open as long as reasonably possible. Your duty is to continue teaching as long as the students are there, and as long as there is calm and order. This is in keeping with the speech, I've checked with the Education Ministry for its correct interpretation and conformation."

Just as suddenly, the PA system is turned off, its noise replaced by a gradual crescendoing murmur hatching questions, paranoiac answers, disgust and fright.

"Tang Li, I just remembered. I've seen this speech before. It's exactly the same one given at Qinghua two years ago when the Red Guards were at our gates."

She finds it incredulous and scrunches her glasses higher up on her nose. "How can you remember or recognize this when it doesn't say anything, unfit for even the pigs?" Tang Li whacks the speech against the armrest between them.

"That's it, that's it exactly, that's why people will remember it."

"What are you saying Ge," Tang Li lowers her voice as they walk near the men from the math department whom she recognizes as Ge's adversaries. "Are you saying everyone's a fool? What about education? How can you believe that and be a teacher, huh?"

The two of them are finally outside the auditorium, but they can't decide if they want to walk over to the hospital or the Geology University to see the grotesque and the carnivalesque, or if they want to avoid bearing witness to China's hemorrhaging. They choose a compromise, and walk toward a tea shop near the university's foreign experts' residency close to the Geology University.

5. THE TEA SHOP

At the tea shop the proprietor asks if they had seen the group of teenagers with red armbands, red hats and red scarves who'd marched down the street earlier that morning.

"They looked a bit threatening," she adds, closing the black notebook she had been entering numbers into and slipping the ballpoint pen into her apron's pocket. "I was walking behind them, being very cautious, trying to decide if I should open the shop."

The only other customer, a thin, older foreign woman with glasses, looks over at them from a shelf of expensive Hainan Island jasmine tea. Tang Li greets her in English but answers the proprietor in Chinese. "Yes, a group of about thirty at the Geology University's side gate. Very rowdy, shouting and waving fists at the lone attendant there."

"Two of the girls were patiently rolling out a sheet of newsprint and a boy was beginning to write some big characters on it, something about a rally," Ge adds, but her attention is on the foreign woman, who is listening intently to this exchange and beginning to walk towards them. "Tang Li," Ge tugs on her friend's sweater. "Tang Li, I think this woman wants to speak to you."

"Hi," she says in English, and now it is Ge who is listening intently, trying to understand with what she can remember of that language from high school. "What's all that commotion in the streets this morning about?"

"You are Joanne, conversation English teacher?"

"Yes, I live in the foreigners' compound just around the corner. What's going on?"

"I think they are the Red Guards looking for trouble," Tang Li points out the shop window in the direction of the Geology University.

"There was a story about them on the VOA this morning," Joanne says, peering out the window. "But I thought they were demonstrating only in the big cities in the south, you know, Beijing, Shanghai and Guangdong? But not up here?"

Joanne is beginning to get visibly nervous. Ge had first heard about these self-effacing fundamentalist Christians in Beijing, and now here in Changchun. Unlike some other foreigners, especially the Germans and Americans, these were quiet and harmless, bringing with them language-learning materials for their students in the sciences and social sciences. They didn't smoke, drink, curse, party or mess around. Their sole vice appeared to be chewing gum. In short, they represented no threat to the political or cultural security of the nation. But once in a while someone's exuberance gets a little carried away. Last spring she heard a rumor that the university's Foreign Affairs Officer had to intervene in their conflict with an American Fulbright Scholar and a Simon Fraser exchange chemistry professor living in the same apartment within the compound. The two had complained that these fundies shouldn't be allowed to hold their revivalist meetings in their common place of residence.

"We just came from a meeting," Tang Li explained. The vice president said we will continue to teach, as long as there are students to teach. But you must be careful; you represent the bourgeoisie, or worse, an icon. They do not understand the difference here."

Ge didn't understand everything Tang Li had said, but she knew enough to warn Joanne in English, "You must go back."

Joanne is stunned. "Go back, I can't go back. I don't have enough money."

"Oh no," Tang Li interrupts. "My friend means go back to the foreigners' compound. She didn't mean America."

"We will walk back with you, safer."

So the three of them leave the tea shop. Outside, the noise level has increased. Several youths are running on the other side of the street, waving sticks and broom handles over their heads. The three women hurry. Around the block at the entrance to the foreigners' compound, the metal gates are locked. Tang Li knocks on them.

"Open up, open up," she yells in Chinese.

A peephole slowly opens, then the gates.

"Bye," Joanne says, turning to Tang Li and Ge before disappearing. "And thank you two very much for explaining everything," she yells from behind the closed gates.

Tang Li and Ge look at each other in silence before walking away from the foreigners' residence, neither one of them saying anything.

"Look where we are," Tang Li points out when they reach the corner of the block.

They had wanted to avoid the commotion and chaos of the teenage crowd, but since they were distracted by their encounter with Joanne, they now find themselves exactly halfway between the hospital and the Geology University.

"There hasn't been a bus all day, Tang Li. We have no choice but to walk north, the long way around."

"It's a pity, that Joanne," Tang Li says. "She's an American, 58 years old, a military secretary all her life, now retired. Her children and husband have dumped her, and her pension isn't enough to live on. I think she became a global, Christian fundamentalist crusader just to make a living. There's nothing spiritual about it; it's a matter of economics, basic survival, subsistence. It's so sad. Global flotsam."

"I think maybe I would do the same thing. It's not hurting anyone."

"Yes, me too. Even so she can't afford to live in America again." Ever the realist, Tang Li continues, increasing her pace.

"The richest country in all of history, and they can't take care of their own people who have worked hard all their lives. She doesn't even have enough money to fly home, see? I heard she was selling some language tapes to her students that she got for free from her embassy in Beijing. Very desperate. I think she will die away from home, in someplace like Changchun, halfway around the world, 10,000 kilometers away from the home of her childhood in Indiana. I would not wish that on anyone. Pity, pity."

Ge looks at the lines in the sidewalk, careful now to avoid stepping on any. She stops Tang Li by tugging on her sweater, turns and, looking straight at her, asks in a gentle voice, "My dear friend, do you think what we do, do you think our teaching will ever make a difference? Tell me." Her body is motionless in the wind that's beginning to pick up.

Tang Li first looks back into Ge's deep brown eyes, then at her firm mouth, then at the cracked line in the sidewalk between them until Ge lets her fingers drop from her sweater. Finally she looks past Ge. "I don't think it ever has, not the way we're supposed to believe. I think the only thing it's ever provided is the unintended opportunity for people to make good friends, sometimes for life."

6. A PARTY

It is like this: twenty seconds of raw terror as she approaches you at a cocktail party. You know what she wants; you'd heard her corner others earlier. She wants to talk about the global diminishing greenhouse's impact on frogs. Have you noticed you don't hear them much anymore? Or she wants to know what you think about the northwestern Indians demonstrating for their right to fish salmon their traditional way with nets. You know that Tippi Hedren, Marlon Brando and Brigitte Bardot support their fish-ins?

It's too late: she has found you. Her smile engages and disarms you and prevents you from making a mad dash for the door, any door.

She says she's Amy and she's from Shreveport, Louisiana, and her father's a shipbuilder and she wants to know what you think about the dam. She's also looking for an ashtray.

What dam, you ask.

"The high dam of course, you're kidding me, you don't know?"

The Hoover, Grand Coulee, Volga, Aswan come to mind and you name them for her even though you know none of them is the one she has in mind.

"No, no, no, no. The one in China. But that's good, at least you'll know what I'm talking about."

She starts to talk about the Gezhouba that's under construction on the Yangtze, but what she really wants to talk about is another one. So you ask.

"They're talking about building another one," she answers, "a bigger one, you know?"

But before you can check yourself, you are already asking, "Which one is that?"

"Oh, that silly dam on the Yangtze, at the last of the Three Gorges, the Xiling."

You are startled by the way her last two words lilt her into another personae. You think it's good Mandarin, for whatever you know about the language, and that's not much, maybe what a third grader knows on an impressive day. Then she tells you this dam was an idea of Sun Yat-sen's in 1919 and again in 1924. Sun, father of China's 20th-century revolution, one of his many, many fathomless ideas. The mish-kid John Hersey wrote a short story about an American engineer who also wanted to build a dam on that river too, at the Witches Gorge, Amy adds.

"What's a mish-kid," you just have to ask.

"Oh, a missionary's kid born in China," Amy explains, not even batting an eyelash. "An MK. Henry Luce, Pearl Buck, maybe Julia Child. A PK, a preacher's kid, is of a lower order."

A decade or so later in 1936, Sun's idea prompted an Austrian hydrologist to travel to the Yangtze, Amy chronicles. And twice in wartime 1944—solicited or not, it's unclear, the first in April and then in May—a John L. Savage, chief design engineer for the US Bureau of Reclamation, took a trip to that river for another feasibility study. Later that year a group of fifty Chinese engineers went to Denver to work with Savage in squirreling away enough hypotheses to prop up a final design for a dam on the Yangtze.

"You don't mean in the middle of the war with a disappearing bank account, Chiang Kai-shek had the gall to initiate a massive irrigation or whatever project?"

"Well, old Peanut Head Chiang wasn't much interested in the war, at least not the war against the Japanese, but that's another matter. Dearie, you should have known that, you being Chinese and all? Oops. You are Chinese aren't you? Someone said you were."

You're getting a little itchy now but vow to pay more attention next time you turn on David Carradine in *Kung Fu*. Maybe you'll learn a little more about being Chinese. Snatch the pebbles from the blind man's hand, Grasshopper, and you'll discover the solution to Fermat's last theorem. You know you won't learn any Mandarin that's spoken all over China now by watching that show. Only Cantonese, remaindered to three places in the world, Hollywood movies, the Bay Area and Hong Kong. Even Beulah Kwok, Keye Luke, Mako, who you suspect is Japanese, all they use is Cantonese, or else it's dubbed in Cantonese.

So, you know, she says, that for a few years the US Bureau of Reclamation officially continued to work on the design of the dam. But it all came to a close when Mao Tse-tung's revolution overtook the country in 1949. A few years later he directed Zhou En-lai to liaise with Nikolai Bulganin for Soviet help. So these translucent Soviet engineers started arriving in China in 1955, along with their grey buildings, grey hats, grey food and grey pencils.

When Mao took his historic long swim across the river at Wuhan in 1956, the plans for the dam became irreversible. He had spoken, citing the dam at the Witches Gorge, and irrevocably committed his words into the equation of a Song Dynasty poetic form a millennium into the feudal past that he abhorred. Imagine that, Amy says, taking a puff on another cigarette, an ugly American and China's *numero uno* revolutionary blueprinting the same vision for China's future, my god!

But the designers under the modernizing Deng Xiaoping, who exhorted the citizenry behind his flaming, five-star red-and-yellow banner proclaiming TO BE RICH IS GLORIOUS, had other ideas and moved the dam site away from the limestone basin of the Witches Gorge to the gneiss or granite or plutonic rock basin of the Xiling Gorge.

There is a pause as she looks at you, so you'll remember, and you will. Deng was the last important who of antecedents to the pronoun they. The rest who followed were exactly that. For instance, the Soviet-trained hydraulic engineer Li Peng, who's the director of Beijing's Electricity Power Administration, and the electrical machinist Jiang Zemin, who's the deputy chief engineer for dynamic mechanics of the Changchun Number One Automobile Plant—each of them a professional politician, neither revolutionary nor reformer nor restorationalist, aka a goddamned bureaucrat or autocrat, same thing—neither has any idea of his own but to sign on the dotted line.

"And there you have it, a short course on the men who dammed the Yangtze."

With a stack of advanced calculus homework that must be graded before 7:30 on Monday and your nagging conflict with teaching math to a group of college kids who don't care about numbers, you just can't hang around for a lecture on dams, Amy or no Amy.

But you know you are just lying to yourself—there is going to be another time. You knew when you first saw her in the room that she will have a place in your life. It could be short, or long, but never a dull moment, you were convinced. But that was before you overheard her discourse on frogs, gillnetting salmon and *the* dam in China before you thought about escaping from her. Now you're not so sure.

These men who are thinking about damming the Yangtze may be an introduction. Then again, it may be just exactly what it is, another man's vanity, but you're stuck in a small mathematics department in a small now-university that used to be a small college until a couple of years ago in a small Wisconsin town without the proper career ambition and too much testosterone, and trying to find an ashtray for a gal from Shreveport, Louisiana, who's talking fast not to be mistook for Vivien Leigh in *Gone with the Wind* and who's really interested in dams on the Yangtze, then and now.

G, pull yourself together. Just go home now before you've had too much to drink. Grade your advanced calculus homework and call Amy in the morning.

7. HOWARD JOHNSON

G is taking a shortcut across the Algoma Bridge to meet Amy at Howard Johnson's for a drink. He is looking at the words on his outside right mirror and trying once more to extrapolate its meaning: *OBJECTS IN MIRROR ARE CLOSER THAN THEY APPEAR*. It's a game he plays to keep himself awake when driving. This time he thinks if that kind of mirror is placed to the side of one's life, in that abstracted and suspended perspective, one will be able to focus clearly on each event as if every layer of ambiguity were slowly peeled away with each scrutiny. Maybe that's why in so many rural living rooms in Wisconsin, Minnesota, South Dakota, Illinois, Iowa, and he suspected Indiana too, large mirrors are hung facing large picture windows, so that people can look not once but twice for the meaning of their lives in such double images, like the reproductions of their loved ones in photographs lining the other walls in their homes. Four children. Fourteen grandchildren. One in college, another in the Marines, Merle's on the JV football team, and Stella's pregnant again. Maybe this is one of the reasons why these states' suicide rates rank among the lowest in the nation, contrasted with those states west of the 100th Meridian. On a clear and smokeless day maybe one can imagine the meaning forever in this doubled reflection. But when

G looks into this mirror tonight and then refocuses to concentrate on swerving onto the exit ramp, he suspects that these residents and their mirrors are wrong, that things only *appear* closer than they really are, making him ever more suspicious of the lives of the people housed in such neat, pastoral landscapes on both sides of the car.

At Howard Johnson's he finds an empty stool at the bar to Amy's left. On her right is her friend Kathy, who is talking to a man whose breath smells of stale beer, peanuts and cigarettes.

"Is he the person you've been waiting for," the man asks, leering at the low-cut fishnet top that Kathy's wearing.

"Yes he is," Amy answers in her sweetest Scarlett O'Hara imitation. "Bartender, bartender, a drink here please. G, scotch, right?"

The man leaves to go to the washroom.

"Whew Amy, who is this guy?"

"You want to ask who is Oshkosh," Kathy leans forward, lifting one of Amy's cigarettes.

G wants to answer, "Silent hunks of people, displaced or not, from Belgium, Holland, Russia, and always Germany, the first illegal aliens, uninvited, who didn't know the language, religion or customs. These translucent men came in unending numbers, their wide-chunked bodies filling their halls, social clubs and churches. Always good with their hands, they now chisel their epitaphs in agonizing alphabets and serve fresh bear stew to everyone up at Fuzzy Thurston's Left Guard Restaurant in Green Bay when the Chicago Bears come to town." Instead, G simply says, "Well I hope he's not looking for trouble," and takes a drink from his glass. "I was a firefighter in the St. Joe National Forest in Idaho, you know."

"He's lying, Kathy. I saw him make up this story last night. It's all books and maps."

The man comes back to the bar and looks straight at G. "This is a pretty small town here, and you must be from the college, right?"

"Yeah, right. Does a bear shit in the woods," G speaks into his drink.

"I hear there're lot of niggars on your football team this year."

G stiffens, sets down his drink, drops his right arm and looks at him. "What d'you say?"

"I said *a lot of niggars on your football team,* you hard of hearing or something?"

Kathy has left to put some quarters into the jukebox, and Amy is pulling on G. "Let it go G, let it go." Petula Clark's *Let It Be Me* joins her from the jukebox.

G is pointing at this man now. "Who the fuck you think you are?"

"... and we don't need your kind either, commie."

The two of them point their fingers at each other's chests now, each jab firmer and deeper. Amy tries to interrupt and get G to dance with her, but it only makes G more determined. When the two men decide to settle it in the parking lot, the bartender reaches for the phone. But before they are out the door, Kathy is at G's side.

"Come dance with me," she says as she steps between them, tall enough to cut off their eye contact, one hand brushing down G's back and the other pulling him onto the dance floor.

G looks over her shoulder at the man disappearing in the company of two guys, and then back at the bar at Amy, who is smiling and nodding. The bartender puts down a fresh scotch in front of G's place, and he too is smiling. Kathy dances real close to G, but in the dim, smoke-filled Oshkosh's Howard Johnson's lounge he is instead thinking about what he saw in the mirror tonight. He wants to point another mirror at their mirror and follow each image back and forth, back and forth until each reversal gets farther and smaller and recedes into nothingness. There he will choose one mirror and place it to the side of their faces to see if it fogs up, if they are still breathing, if anything is still alive in there.

8. VIEW FROM THE ROOF

We all became orphans.
(Leslie Silko, *Almanac of the Dead*)

Ge's on the roof of the four-story languages and literature building with Tang Li and her husband Xie and their binoculars. On a slight rise, it's one of the tallest buildings in eastern Changchun, so they can see the entrances to both the hospital and the Geology University, at least the lighted gates where the teenagers are gathered.

"They're getting ready to do something," Xie says, pointing to the group at the university. One of his organic chemistry students had told him, he continues, that some of the group leaders, boys no older than sixteen or seventeen, had boasted about entering and searching more than ten bourgeois families' homes the previous night, confiscating pictures, cameras, books and a foreign language typewriter, all in the name of cultural cleansing. After their search, these teenagers had changed the menus in some Muslim restaurants, substituting pork for beef. "That must be them," he whispers, handing the binoculars to Ge.

She refocuses the lens on the taller boys in front of a group of other teenagers, all wearing something red, in front of the closed gate. He is shouting and making an exaggerated effort of lifting his left arm, his right hand carefully drawing back the coat's sleeve. Ge hears cheering when the boy reveals the confiscated watches that circle his scrawny arm all the way to the biceps.

"They're leaving," Tang Li nudges Ge. "They're going away."

But they're not dispersing, just heading towards Stalin Boulevard, away from the residential neighborhood, yelling and waving. Occasionally someone stops under a street lamp and picks up something from the sidewalk and stows it in his pocket or the bag he's carrying.

At the hospital on the other side of the wide boulevard, a different group of teenagers has started singing. Ge, Tang Li and her husband Xie think they can actually hear the words when the wind is right. Through the binoculars Ge sees that the leader is the same girl who publicly cut her pigtails last week. Tonight she is hatless and wearing a red scarf.

"Some of them might be our students in a year or two," someone mutters, but Ge cannot be sure if Xie or his wife has said it.

"And later they'll become intellectuals like us," Ge says, "people who don't work with their hands, who do not lift, pull, push, twist, hammer, choke or punch."

"That's right Ge, now you're talking like one of the homeless ones down there." It is Tang Li who has said it.

"Talk, talk, talk, that's all we ever do," Ge continues. "We're cowards, but we act like tyrants when the political situation permits, don't we? Isn't that what Confucianism is all about? And we've been doing this for more than two thousand years."

"I'm just an organic chemist," Xie interrupts. "Leave me out of this."

"What are you talking about," Tang Li looks at her husband and raises her voice. "Like an engineer, musician or even a mathematician," she says, pointing to Ge, "You're among the worst. You're totally apolitical, and among the first to surrender and cry *Uncle* and sell out, even before the farmers."

A convoy of cars moves up Stalin Boulevard and stops in front of the Public Security Bureau building, the beams from the headlamps forming tiny conicals of light next to the bluish glow of the streetlamps.

Xie focuses his binoculars on the lead car. "It's a Red Flag limo, and it's got the special white plates with the red *GA* and black numbers. Top security. Very powerful. And look, look who's getting out," Xie hands Ge the binoculars. "It's Jiang Zemin, I've seen his picture in the newspapers. One of the top leaders at the Number One Automobile Plant. Some say he's not really a mechanical engineer but a bureaucrat, someone who dreams of having his butt screwed to a chair until death, wearing a fountain pen in his jacket pocket, official stamps in both hands, who can't ever give a speech without crib notes, hah, hah."

"Yes, those same thick, black plastic frames," Ge looks through the binoculars. A future czar in a Soviet fur hat in a chauffeured limousine surrounded by the best security Changchun can muster. "I don't like this man, I never have. He looks like a cadaver done up by a mortician who flunked basic formaldehyde." Several others have also come out of their cars, some side armed in the green uniform with the red epaulets and gold bars from the Ministry of Public Security. "They look pretty severe. Jiang looks perturbed and disgusted, and he seems to be yelling at someone who isn't there, that arrogant son-of-a-pig. No one has come out of the PSB building, and there's no light inside that I can see from here."

All at once the officials return to their cars, and the convoy makes a U-turn at the next crossing and returns south on the boulevard. It disappears in a turn onto the street that would take it out of the city into the well-guarded and exclusive residence of the powerful, top party officials at South Lake.

"They never saw the two groups of teenagers on both sides of them," Ge returns the binoculars to Xie. "Amazing, simply amazing. There's the history of ideological struggle in 20th-century China right there, don't you see? Every piece is in place."

"What are you talking about," Xie asks.

"The youth, the powerful leaders who choose to ignore them or use them, same thing, the institutions of education and health care serving as a playground for the ideological struggle, or what appears to be a conflict, but it's not, because there's no real struggle for anything when the powerful leadership holds everything in its fists."

Xie is amazed at his wife's answer and his mouth opens to say something, but he is speechless.

"Yes, yes," Ge gets into it, gesturing with her hands. "China is not a communist country but really a fascist nation led by a communist party."

"You're saying that the real crooks in China get away with anything they want since they moonlight by running the country?"

"Yes, Xie," Tang Li answers. "Now you've got it. Not bad for an organic chemist."

"And everyone else must blend in, blend in because the goose that flies in front of the flock will be shot? *Qiangda chutou niao!*"

"Or to the sides or at the end too, hah, hah," Ge giggles.

And then Xie says it for all three of them. "That's why they're called the Red Guards, these teenagers are the guards. They're anti-feudal, anti-imperialist; but they also learn fast because in a minute everything is reversed and misunderstood and confused and they begin to wield the little power they're allowed by targeting the same geese they're meant to guard ..."

"Oh stop it Xie," Tang Li interrupts. "Stop it. This is going too far. When is a white horse ever going to be just a white horse in China; when is a red wheelbarrow ever going to be just a red wheelbarrow?"

"In China," Ge stops to laugh. "In China, a white horse is never a white horse," she added. Then Tang Li laughs, then Xie, all three of them orphaned here to this chilly late-October night on the roof of Changchun's Jilin University's languages and literature building. And who isn't?

The squad of Red Guard #2 has crossed Stalin Boulevard and reached the hospital where a smaller squad of Red Guard #1 has stopped singing. Someone has found a rock in his hand and hefts it in his fist before taking careful aim and flinging it at the forehead of the nearest opposing guard across the street.

9. UNLISTED NUMBER

G was never a firefighter in Idaho's St. Joe National Forest. In fact he's never been a firefighter, or to the St. Joe, or Idaho, or anywhere west of the 100th Meridian. As a freshman at MIT, he had thought about applying there for a summer job because the pay was good. Instead, he got a job waiting tables in downtown Boston at the Ritz facing the Public Gardens across the Longfellow Bridge where the tips were good. Instead, he is now poring over maps of Idaho looking for schools he would like to teach at, or just places where he would like to spend a future summer vacation when his meager salary allowed: the River of No Return, maybe prompted by the movie of the same name he saw when he lived in Cambridge, Simmons Peak Lookout, University of Idaho, and then maybe a jaunt into Washington, the Potholes, whatever they are, the behemoth Grand Coulee Dam in the middle of Indian country now turned into a recreational area. Instead, he is imagining the identity of a firefighter in the St. Joe National Forest for himself, as he had done two nights ago when Amy was over.

G picks up the ringing telephone.

"I think you should know there's going to be some trouble."

It is Joyce Hunter. Even though his number is unlisted, G

doesn't say anything. At its November meeting last week, the Student Senate had deadlocked on accepting the Black Student Union's enabling charter, but the tie had been broken by the Senate's president, David Frank. G had noticed that most of the opposition came from the Greeks, from Alpha to Omega, and a strange coalition of wannabe Junior Leaguers, who then sat open-mouthed as Frank, a fellow Caucasian, argued for the recognition of the BSU. From the anger these student senators displayed at the end of the meeting, G knew there was going to be trouble.

When he left that meeting he thought about those students, and how the country's intellectuals, including its teachers, are entrusted with propping up the entire middle class, perpetuating a vast cultural infrastructure built on everything it has co-opted. These are their pissant children he has to teach. How can he teach them anything when they don't even know who they are? No wonder the man said, *Forgive them, for they do not know what they do.* How can anyone know what they've done if they don't even know *a priori* who they are, and most of his students do not.

So G went back to his apartment and opened a bottle of scotch, which made things worse.

"So all we do is talk, talk, talk among ourselves in the middle of the night," he said to Amy over the phone as he looked at his watch. "We don't do anything to make a real difference; we are cowards and suck on our daily ration of 400 lies, like everyone else. I should be at your place fucking on your 310-thread count cotton sheets and again in the morning maybe on the kitchen table or in the shower; but instead we're on the phone at two in the morning talk, talk, talk, and first thing I'll do tomorrow morning is jump up and head straight for my 7:30 DE class in Clow. There's got to be something else we can do with our lives. You should've seen the anger and rage in their eyes tonight."

So G is not surprised at what Joyce is now saying on the phone. "What kind of trouble," he asks.

"We're going to present the list of demands to President Roger Guiles at Dempsey tomorrow morning, in person."

G wants to say *You're crazy to think he's even going to be awake in the morning—people like him are known to go from the cradle to the grave without ever opening an eyelid,* but manages to ask, "What makes you think Jolly Roger's going to be in his office," grateful that he's on the phone and Joyce can't see his smirk.

"You are my professor..."

"Your instructor."

"You are my instructor, but you are so slow, or forgetful. Remember? I'm good at keeping my ear to the ground; I've been doing it for 300 years?"

But G remembered before Joyce had answered, and is instead thinking about the list of four demands hand-delivered to President Guiles's office two weeks ago: 1) place the black experience in the curriculum; 2) recruit black faculty members; 3) establish an Afro-American cultural center; 4) secure funds to furnish the center and promote the black experience. At the BSU meeting the night before, there was argument over adding a fifth item, one calling on university officials to apply pressure on downtown barbers to cut the black students' hair, but that thought had surfaced after midnight when any new idea would have been deep fried, canned or rolled into a tear of cigarette paper and smoked, and was.

"8:30 tomorrow?"

This Joyce is too much. But wait, G thinks. The Thursday morning just before Thanksgiving break might be the right moment, catch everyone with the expectation of leaving, and at 8:30 in the morning they might just find everyone in a public educational institution less nasty, from the groundskeeper to the president. So he says, "I'll be there, 8:30, Dempsey."

Click! This is the fourth time in the conversation G has heard this background noise in their phone conversation, and since the second one he's timed the intervals evenly at 30 seconds. "Joyce, Joyce, is there someone on an extension?"

"No, I'm calling from a pay phone. Why?"

"Okay, I thought, did you hear... I'll see you tomorrow morning. And keep your ears to the ground."

"Ear, G, one ear. How can anyone put two ears to the ground?"

G hangs up and stands a moment looking about his apartment, but he isn't sure what he's looking for, or what he's looking at. He wonders who's keeping an ear to his phone, but he already knows the answer to that. He lights up a cigarette and walks into the kitchen as if he's walked through a peephole into a totalitarian landscape expecting to be examined limb by limb, time after time, his every gaze surrounded by windows showing nothing on the other side but the hacking, rusted sound of being recorded on moving magnetic tape.

If they're going to get me, there's nothing I can do to prevent it, he concludes, smiling and reaching for his scotch and ice, wishing he had a wingman, an angel on his blind side, but he knows he doesn't, no one in Oshkosh ever does.

10. THE TANK

In the last two days, the hospital by Stalin Boulevard has become a battleground, Red Guard #1 against Red Guard #2. Most of Changchun's residents have been able to go about their business by avoiding this area, and parents of teenagers have made discrete, indirect and unsuccessful attempts at keeping their former children home, but some of them haven't been seen in days, not even at mealtimes. The primary and secondary schools? Their gates closed and locked, the teachers have gone into hiding. With groups of teenagers roaming around town looking for targets of revenge, some with sticks, some with red banners, even the groundskeepers who usually live in the schools' gatehouses have disappeared, along with the principals and librarians and the PSB police.

This has meant that Ge needs thirty more minutes to get to campus, where some students are still showing up for their classes. Most of the class time has focused on separating rumor from lore, report from fantasy. When her students discovered that more could be learned in her beginning calculus class about the Red Guard activities downtown and word got out, more started showing up, including some who weren't even her students. Ge made no pretense of working with them on some calculus problem, and instead would sit at a student's desk in the back of the classroom looking out a window, wondering if she should have gone into something else, like medicine or genetics. Would the same, exact thing be happening if she had?

A week ago the teenagers of Red Guard #1 had hung a banner outside the first-story windows of the hospital, on the street side, declaring it the *CHANGCHUN COMMUNE*. Rocks started flying immediately from the Red Guard #2 contingent outside the building, but they were useless as Red Guard #1 had retreated to the second and third floors. The two bed-confined patients had been evacuated easily enough by four thoughtful boys, who returned an hour later armed with two ancient WWII Japanese rifles and several rounds of ammunition which had been hidden for thirty some years still wrapped in their original waxed paper. At the same time Red Guard #2 had acquired some still functioning black-marketed British Enfields with a handful of shells, to even the odds in the escalating conflict.

"When the shooting started, I quickly ducked around the corner," said the student with this scoop.

But it was over in less than a minute, the supply of bullets had been emptied, and no one hit. And then it was back to the rocks again. When Red Guard #1 ran out of the rocks they had carried into the building, they started tearing down the inside walls of the hospital piece by piece, their endless supply of warring materiel.

"Did you see the leader of Red Guard #1, the girl with the short hair," Ge had asked from her window seat.

When Red Guard #2 concluded that it was impossible to mount a successful assault on the hospital, its members then took over and occupied the Jilin Province Government Building on the other side of the street. Day and night, stones, rocks, pieces of chipped mortar and sometimes small bottles would rain down onto Stalin Boulevard from the rooftops of these buildings for no reason at all, as if these teenagers wanted reassurance that the basic law of gravity was still working.

"Well, at least this changes the legacy of combat between the Japanese and British rifles on a main street in China named after a Soviet leader," Tang Li said when Ge told her the story later that afternoon. "Now we're killing each other, like we have so many times this century, 1911, 1919, 1927, you want me to go on? I also heard the rumor last night that two Beijing Red Guard advisors had arrived to organize and coordinate its national efforts, but when they heard what was going in Changchun, they were so horrified by tales of provincial and self-destructive conflicts, they took the very next train home."

At this moment, the two of them are walking back to their apartments. Xie had joined them as they walked past the chemistry building, but then went ahead to pick up some fish at the market. Now he's back, shaking his head.

"You won't believe this," he says, showing the paper that had been used to wrap the fish. "Look at this, it's the perforated computer paper outlining the maintenance record of a vintage Soviet MiG-15 now guarding the skies of Changchun."

Ge looks down at the partially torn paper, the serial number, dates of production and transfers, and service history. But before she has time to read the row of numbers at the bottom of the page, she hears a low, metallic grinding noise coming around the corner.

Is it a diesel truck that's about to break down and fall apart? Is it a partially assembled tractor from the factory? It's coming from the direction of the Changchun Technology and Industry College.

"Those mechanical engineering students have made an imitation Norinco tank!" Xie yells.

It's a monster—heavy sheet metal covering most of its four sides, including the tires. A long pipe is sticking out of what appears to be its front. It moves slowly, the metal plates banging against its sides. Dark smoke pours out its back. It is a dragon, and it's going to parade down Stalin Boulevard, demanding recognition, all of China's vanity calcified in the illusion of this moment.

Ge begins counting slowly, 2, 3, 5, 7, 11, 13, 17, 19, 23. At 199 she whispers a promise to herself that she'll be leaving Changchun, and at 251 she knows that it'll happen before this semester's out.

11. HERTZ RENTALS

> *Heroic children, with unexampled courage they*
> *threw themselves at the tanks, gasoline bombs in*
> *hand, and carried dispatches under a hail of bullets.*
> (Anna Swirszczyñska, "Building the Barricade")

At 8:45 the next morning Joyce is not keeping her ear to the
ground. She's not even in her 7:30 DE class that she never misses.
She's upstairs in front of Dempsey-200 with the other BSU
students trying to talk past Dr. Gunderson, President Roger E.
Guiles's gatekeeper, to present their demands to the president
personally. (Some say that Dr. Gunderson's job description
includes keeping the president's eyelids open from time to time.)
Overwhelmed by their numbers, he steps aside, and a few students
enter D-200, the president's reception area. Two of them knock
on Guiles's private office and enter without waiting for an answer.

He is sitting at his desk. By now both his eyes are wide open,
and the letter with the demands is presented to him. Next month
he will testify in court to being the victim of undesirable actions
in his office: *I looked up somewhat surprised to find students standing*
in the doorway or moving through the doorway. I looked up and asked
if they had an appointment. As I looked again, I noticed that they were

in front of a much larger group of persons, who moved in through the office until there seemed to be no more space available. I was presented with an eight-and-a-half-by-eleven size sheet of paper on which were listed a number of demands, and I was told that I was expected to sign the statement.

G has ended his 7:30 DE class early and is outside the building with Amy and some other instructors and a few non-BSU students, and looking up, they can see the shapes of several persons entering the president's suite. There is purpose to their gestures and movements, and soon G hears intermittent shouting, and the muffled crash of falling objects.

One student has knocked over a filing cabinet, spilling the secreted files of forty years of unread, rolling assessments of the effectiveness of the university's general education courses required of every student. Another picks up the black phone with the shoulder rest, listens to it, then yanks its cord from the wall. Someone fixes on the secretary's robin-egg blue IBM Selectric typewriter, picks it up and walks it over to the window.

Downstairs, everyone hears the window crash and ducks quickly, the typewriter sinking into the lawn muddy from last night's rain, its electric cord resembling a long rat's tail. There is nothing G and the others standing around the half-buried typewriter can do but wait for things to take their shape. A crow quietly flies away from the upper branches of a nearby elm.

In less than fifteen minutes the demonstration is over, leaving behind a bewildered president, a trashed phone and typewriter, a couple of broken ashtrays, a chair with a broken arm, and a knocked-over filing cabinet. The sum of damage to the state of Wisconsin taxpayers: $429.89.

But the BSU students do not leave Dempsey. They're hanging around, talking with other administrators about their demands when the law arrives, the combined force of four enforcement agencies in their squad cars, vans and three Hertz rental trucks pulling up one-way Algoma from the wrong direction. A two-minute dispersal warning is given repeatedly over a bullhorn, but no one seems to be listening.

Modern history is packed with chronicles of nations periodically aborting their young in events cataclysmic or anemic, throwing away their children into exile, or worse, lifelong bitterness. Sometimes these are recorded by the world press or Amnesty International, but more often our eyes are suddenly averted, the exchange of unrelenting silence between strangers and bystanders conspiring to bear no witness to anyone's hurt. Such upheavals have occurred in both China and the United States, and this narrative involving 104 American teenagers in Oshkosh, Wisconsin, on this Thursday, November 21, 1968, does not go beyond the pages of the *Milwaukee Journal* ninety miles to the south.

Each of the 104 students are individually handcuffed and led out of Dempsey into the awaiting Hertz rental trucks, up the gangplanks and into the dark cargo holds without windows or light. Joyce turns and looks for G in the gathering throng. He sees in her eyes the recognition of another voyage taken 300 years ago. She is listening.

12. ACTIVISM

Charged with rioting, destruction of property and resisting arrest, these students are delivered to the Winnebago County Court House where they're first booked, and then at 1:30 arraigned before Judges Sitter and Miller, and later Judges Channey and Horowitz, in groups of five. By 3:00 they are on their way to jail. Because of the limited size of these local lockups, the students are then transferred to different jails in four separate counties:

Winnebago County Jail
    Lonnie E. Woods
    Bradley Thurman
    Darryl Bevly
    Jerry Benston
    Robert Willis
    Ernest Abbott
    Samuel J. Henly
    Elmer H. Jackson — *note to guards: parole, do not release*
    Robert Hayes
    Thomas A. Miles
    Vince Bevenue
    Michael Gordon

Kenneth E. Owens
Lamont Robbins
Michael Carufel
Jerrel L. Malone
Henry W. Browne III
Joel Johnson
Caleb Leggett
Henry L. Clay
Carl Carroll
Philipp Hardin*
Charles E. Kimble—juvenile
Willie M. Sinclair—juvenile
Judy Braggs—juvenile
Susette Gordo—juvenile
Rita P. Johnson—juvenile
Gloria J. Palmer—juvenile
B. Rodgus—juvenile*

Neenah Police Department Jail

Edward Franks Jr.
Ross Grant
Anthony Brunson
Milton Mitchell
Manuel Cockroft
Gregory M. Doby

Fond du Lac County Jail

Ervin L. Weatherby
Richard Browne
Leonard C. White Jr.
Bernard Patterson
Rufus E. Finner
Jarden Eckles
James R. Tatum
Roger Hanson*
Allan J. Guiffre*

Outagamie County Jail

Geoffrey W. McCreary
Jeffrey Maurar*
Donald S. Jackson

    Charles Stern*
    George R. North
    Robert Martin
    Alvin Taylor*
    James Allen
    Glen E. Davis
    Jesse J. Miller III

Waushara County Jail
    Glenn Ross
    Robert J. Harris
    Glenn E. Ferguson
    Elliott Ross

Location unspecified in booking report
    Joyce A. Hunter
    Carolyn J. Warren
    Margaret Bell
    Yvonne Gransberry
    Janice Brazil
    Delores Banks
    Essie Reed
    Karen D. Berkley
    Phyllis M. Graham
    Kate I. Gray
    Gay Howard
    Shirley Johnson
    Karen M. Williams
    Barbara Adams
    Sandra K. McCreary
    Vada R. Harris
    Cheime Brown*
    Celeste Campbell
    Susan M. Woodruff
    Sandra J. Bendra
    Gladys Coleman
    Sandy Calvin
    Dorothy J. Palmer
    Mary Barnes
    Loretta Mattox

Floria Bell
Juanita D. Moore
Lyna M. Johnson
Carolyn Staples
Ruth A. King
Martha Leonard
Bettye J. McCadney
Irma D. Hall
Sheila J. Morgan
Vicki C. Marzette
Avera Wilson
Wanetta J. Fullove
Rhonda L. Foulks
Ruth L. Frausto
Barbara J. Dallas
Noreen A. Debnam

non BSU student

Sum of damage that will be billed to the state of Wisconsin taxpayers: another rent in the heart, another mortgage over the conscience, another shame. Just before Christmas, Federal District Judge James E. Doyle will write that *the events cannot be recounted without evoking deep sadness; sadness in the memory of decades, even centuries, of injustice, the fruits of which are now so insistently with us; sadness that this legacy seems now to be producing a profound sickness in some of our people.*

13. THE BACKLASH

In working with Milwaukee attorney and state representative Lloyd Barbee first for bail for these students, then later their legal defense, and still later responding to the students' summary suspension from the university for

> a) interference with the administrative functions and activities of the university,
> b) without authority occupy university facilities and block access to the areas in Dempsey Hall, and
> c) infringe upon the rights of students, faculty, staff and authorized persons to gain access to university facilities,

G has problems determining the precise number of students affected. The university has no accurate record, nor the law enforcement agencies. The number fluctuates between 86 and 110. G suspects a few of the names he sees on the lists are duplications, some not members of the BSU but WASP supporters and SDS members, others non-students from Milwaukee, Madison and South Beloit who came up to Oshkosh in solidarity.

In the meantime Barbee is asking Judge James V. Sitter in

the US District Court for the Western District of Wisconsin to disqualify himself from listening to a restraining order request against the university and its regents from summarily expelling these students without a hearing, on the grounds that Sitter had earlier used the word *nigger* in a burglary case in his court. A bigot can't rule on this case!

Congratulations for the university's decision to bring in the police. Petitions for the administrators to expel the students and press criminal charges against them start arriving from everywhere. First a Western Union telegram from the Sharon Singstock of the class of '65 or '66, G isn't sure which, an Alpha Phi who later became Miss Wisconsin, now the proprietor of San Francisco's Mama Sing's School of Chinese Cooking. Clever, very clever.

Two Kiwanis Clubs add their voices to other area civic groups praising the strict and swift action of WSU-O president Jolly Roger, the Lakeshore Kiwanis Club and the Kiwanis Club of Oshkosh.

Under the leadership of Robert Yarbro, the Oshkosh Area Chamber of Commerce begins circulating one thousand petitions seeking the immediate and permanent expulsion of the black student protesters.

And brothers of the local chapter of a fraternity send a letter to the editor of the *Oshkosh Daily Northwestern*:

> *To the Editor:*
>
> *Open letter to the Oshkosh Police department.*
>
> *We, the brothers of Sigma Pi fraternity at WSU-O, would like to thank the Oshkosh Police department for the excellent job they did at the recent Negro demonstrations at the University.*
>
> *Not only did you do a superb job of protecting the innocent students, professors, and administrators who were trapped in Dempsey Hall at the time of the melee, but we feel that you also performed a valuable service*

by protecting the student prisoners from what could have been a dangerous mob of irate students.

We are fortunate to be students in a city where the Police department is as efficient, professional, and considerate as yours.

Thank you once again.

Timothy J. Morrissey
Corresponding secretary
Sigma Pi fraternity, WSU-O

14. LEAVING

We were departing in order to leave,
leaving in order to leave some more,
some more tired, some more old.
(Li-Young Lee, *The Winged Seed*)

In a warm, sun-drenched Sunday afternoon unusual for Changchun in early December, Ge is taking a walk with Tang Li in their neighborhood park. Life has been back to normal since the Red Guards juggernaut was broken a week ago by the techies dragon, the teenagers off the streets, and the PSB back on the beat, in that order.

"Life, after all, doesn't have to be all bad, even in Changchun," Tang Li points to the blue sky in her new, broad embroidered sleeves.

Ge asks about the American teacher Joanne, who's doing well, still selling language tapes she gets free from the embassy in Beijing. But they both know that this might be the last time they will be talking like this in Changchun. They understand each other, and they have no need to talk about it—Tang Li and Xie will walk Ge to the rail station next week and say goodbye, and there will be no tears—their generation has experienced too many degrees of separation.

"You must be careful in Beijing," Tang Li could not help herself.

"*Xie xie*, thank you. I will just stop overnight to see professor Luo one more time. The Red Guards have lost their steam, and only Jiang Qing is left prattling about."

"Yes, but she is not harmless, you know that. As Mao's wife, she still wields considerable power." Tang Li then describes Jiang Qing's involvement in structuring the Ministry of Culture as the watchdog of China's arts, making sure every poem, painting and dance serves the ideological currency of the party, like its preposterous Soviet model. "She's not just the innocent banning of one thousand operas in the name of state security."

"My friend, such a worrier. I'll be in Beijing for only one day, then I'll be on another train for Chengdu where my cousin lives. I'm more worried about getting a job."

"Maybe you'll teach a bit there before you find something else?"

"No, my friend, I don't think so. There's absolutely no acceptable collective or personal purpose to continue teaching left in me. I'll find something in Chengdu, don't worry. I'll give you my cousin's phone number."

They both stop talking and look upward to see four geese flying overhead, the fourth beginning to falter behind.

Ge stops and looks over at Tang Li. "Don't you dare. Don't you dare make a national metaphor out of that. It's just four geese flying overhead, and the last one is tiring."

They burst out laughing, their merriment forming roots as deep as their trust in each other, and together they look up and follow the geese fading into the southern horizon.

15. LAST CLASS

For the first time G is late for his 7:30 DE class in Clow—another middle-of-the-night phone conversation with Amy has thrown him off his routine. The phone was ringing at one when he finally got back to his apartment after preparing next week's legal strategy with Lloyd Barbee, who'd brought along his Milwaukee neighbor Ajax the White Knight, Father Groppi, for inspiration. Amy wanted to know how G was doing and tried to discourage him from quitting teaching, a decision he made when he found out that the ever-apolitical math department of male basketball half-court players had sent a letter of support to WSU-O's administration.

By example from her literary map, she said, "We've had traitors too you know. You know, G, that our country's had a long history of writers and poets who served the fascist currency: Ezra Pound, Edward Weismiller, Whittaker Chambers, Owen Lattimore, Jack Kerouac and maybe Archibald MacLeish too, not to mention Richard Ellman, Norman Pearson, Donald Gallup, Louise Martz, and some would even include the defector, T.S. Eliot too." But Amy was not convincing enough; G has been approaching this decision for more than a year.

The students are all here this morning and very attentive to

G. When he passes out the graded homework, for the first time in his short teaching career of one long year at South Dakota and an even longer partial semester at Oshkosh, the students' eyes continue their intense focus on him instead of their grades, checking him out for the slightest twinge of betrayal, ready to report any transgression to the chair of the department. All math majors now since Joyce is not here, and all white since Joyce is not here, her seat empty in the second row to the left, they own it all.

G feels it and resists the impulse to put on his sunshades. The door to his classroom clicks open, and all eyes shift to its small opening. But it's not small enough to hide the grey frame of academic vice president Ray "Rocket" Ramsden, a clipboard with a list of classes, timetables and instructor names superglued to his left hand and a pencil in his right. He's stalking every corridor of every classroom building making sure every instructor is sticking to the course content and not discussing opposition to the war in Vietnam or participation in the voter registration drive in Mississippi, and today, three days after December 7, that no taxpayer-salaried official is informing the state's children that there will be an informational teach-in on the November 21 incident and its subsequent events later that day. Or else. Or else he will place a pencil check next to their names for retribution later. No siree. Not on his watch.

There are smiles on G's students' faces, except for the only remaining student sitting in the front row, a bright and promising out-of-state whiz-kid from Lincoln-country Illinois, Alix Houston. The sound from the nickel-plated tongue latching back into place in the door handle reverberates into an echo, an echo that lasts and becomes the life-changing, essential gesture or grimace or glance of unwhisperable things that will remain forever.

G looks at the empty space in the second row, to his left, the one Joyce has left. Everyone in the classroom looks at it. He feels a rage developing. *I can't continue teaching these students anymore. Their fathers are members of animal clubs, the Elks, the Eagles, the Lions, the Moose. They send letters of congratulations to Jolly Roger and urge him to do more, rah-rah-rah, we're number one. They want to hang John Carlos and Tommie Smith for their gloved, black salute at last summer's Olympics in Mexico City, take away their passports and ship them home. These crackers volunteer their number to the top of the draft to go to the Iwo Jimas and Koreas and Vietnams to join the British or the French or the Germans or the Aussies and pull the trigger on their M-1s or M-15s or M-16s or Enfields or Springfields or Garands or BARs or service Colts or whatever, just like squeezing a lemon; or deploy napalm or fragmentation-bomb or poison or mine and drop bouncing-betties or daisy cutters or CBU-55s or CBU-87/B CEMs with 200 two-pound parachuted bomblets; or pick up 235 or 238 or plutonium from the uranium pile and nuke the other—who could-have-been me, my family of families—back to the stone age. Every man, woman and child for future insurance. They do this and more while their families erect indiscriminate cemeteries or monuments to honor them, their thank-you card, we're so proud of you, sorry you aren't here. He straightens up, his eyes scanning their faces. What am I doing here? These students in front of me are their pissant children, and I am helping them grow up to be just like their pissant parents.*

G feels exhausted and wants out. He walks over to the nearest window and heaves its frame up to a cool, Wisconsin December morning 27 years late. "Fuck you; fuck you Oshkosh," he yells at the top of his lungs. He then turns and walks right past his students, their mouths agape, right out of the classroom, out of Clow, out of Oshkosh and out of teaching forever.

Part Two

*True connoisseurs, however, are known to favor the
stretch in between, since it's the hardest to do anything with.*
(Margaret Atwood, "Happy Endings")

Chengdu, 1972

16. ANCIENT OBSERVATORY

Ge has been here almost four years now. Going by train from Changchun to Beijing had been relatively simple, an 18-hour ride with only one change in Shenyang. But the travel from Beijing to Chengdu was another story, a long and hard trip of almost two days. Had Professor Luo not been there to help her find the right ticket office in Beijing, she might still be looking for it, since she knew from her seven years of student days that most people in Beijing did not know directions beyond their most immediate neighborhood.

Professor Luo was waiting for Ge at the Main Railway Station platform when her train pulled in on that early December morning. Looking more relaxed than she remembered him from four years ago, he had a warm smile and a present for her. Ge set down her bags and slowly untied the red ribbon and unfolded the white tissue paper to a Qinghua University PhD-in-finite-numbers diploma with all the appropriate signatures and official stamps.

"*Xie xie*," she said, looking up at him, a whisper of light gathering behind her eye. "You have always been here for me; I will always remember that."

"*Xie xie*," she thanked him again a moment later, and reached out to touch him, thankful for his caring. But it wasn't like that, you see. The professor was her dear, dear friend, the net below the precipice, the rope along a catwalk.

Together the two of them carried all her belongings and trudged over to the hidden ticket office at the east loop of Qianmen Lu but set back from the theater fronting the street. With about five hours before the Chengdu train's departure, they decided to walk over to the Ancient Observatory.

Except for the six or seven attendants on the main floor who appeared to have been napping at ten in the morning, the place was deserted.

"For some reason the children had left this building alone," Professor Luo said. By refusing to refer to them as *The Red Guards,* he thought he could diminish their importance and wish them away; by referring to them as *children,* he thought he could forget the damage to people and property that others had moved them to do. But how can he forget that? What he really wanted everyone to acknowledge, damn it, what he really wanted to say, damn it, was that these children were someone else's surrogate. They only did what their parents wanted to do but did not dare to — so they connived and manipulated their pissant children into doing it. Damn it, why is it so hard for anyone to say something direct in China! Instead, he said to Ge, and answered his own question, "Perhaps this was one of the buildings protected by Zhou Enlai."

On the rooftop after the steep climb, Beijing opened up to them, a breath of fresh air on a borrowed day. Here in this elevated open space above Beijing, Ge found rest from her life and imagined she could see the shadow of the Great Wall to the north and face the truth of her own life. "Lao Luo," she used the endeared form of address. "Lao Luo, I've quit teaching. I respect and admire what you do, but I can't do it any more — it's not right for me."

Professor Luo turned toward the north, as if he too could see the dark shape of the Great Wall. "I know," he said, removing his glasses and cleaning them with the hem of his sweater.

"I've lost the sense of purpose in teaching," Ge continued. "I want to do something else, something I can believe in."

"Well Ge, if you want to stay in mathematics, especially in finite numbers, teaching in the university is the only place. Anywhere else they'll want results, applications, even in America."

"I've done some checking around, there's not much left after the government or the military. Even there it's pretty much complex computations, code work or security contingencies for the PLA. Some Fortran, some Cobalt, that's about it, especially for a woman."

"Of course you're right." Professor Luo stopped to look around the roof. "You saw the early astronomical and navigational instruments downstairs, those used in the 15th, 16th and 17th centuries for navigation and meteorology. Here on the roof," his right arm sweeping a circumference around them, "there's that equatorial armilla, celestial globe, altazimuth—this is where the French Jesuits parlayed the calculations prize they won from the Muslims into an Imperial Bureau of Astronomy appointment."

Yes, yes, you already know, ahead of the other Catholics, and by the 19th century, over thirty competing Protestant sects, including the Baptists, Southern Baptists, Presbyterians, Lutherans, Methodists, Episcopalians, and Wesleyans, sometimes masked under such educational institutions as Yale or Harvard or Missouri or Johns Hopkins from the United States, and others from just about every other European nation, and now, in 1972 after Richard Nixon's visit, they are poised at Tulsa, Pasadena and Salt Lake City, ready to thump their Bibles across the new China.

"I remember, *practicing evidential research.* Hard, meticulous, discrete data collected with rigorous ant-like precision. A change from the speculative, metaphysical and sometimes riskier moralistic models. It was hell on the state exams in the 18*th* century. A lot of suicides and beheadings. What a period for mathematics here and around the world!"

They walked over to the azimuth theodolite covered with sculpted bronze dragons. "Results and applications aren't always so bad," Professor Luo said, smiling up at Ge, one hand trailing along the ridge of a vexing dragon. "Someone has to do it, and only a few can do it right. It doesn't always have to end in a rifle or a cannon."

On the long train ride to Chengdu, Ge had almost two full days to remember this conversation, the hard, cold window seat emphasizing Professor Luo's last comment on the observatory roof. During daylight hours, she could almost translate the passing rural landscape into a mathematical language she has yet to understand; and at night, little by little, the dots of village lights merged into remembered lines trailing behind the few vague raindrops collected on the moving windowpane. Here she looked forward to meeting Chengdu, the Chengdu she hoped would endure as a landing place.

Pittsburgh, 1972

17. AT THE DUMPSTER

That's a good question, how G got here after he told Oshkosh to fuck off. At least he didn't have to struggle with what grades to give his students who'd, a) been canned by the university because they were black, like Joyce, or b) disappeared from his class for weeks on a voter registration drive in Mississippi, or c) faded into the SDS or more radical network. Had he given them *F*s, every conventional head would have sided with him, including the math department chair, dean, vice president, president, both Kiwanis and brothers of Sigma Pi. Had he given them *A*s, as G was inclined, there would have been all hell to pay—oh yeah, the long reach of those self-appointed defenders of the faith. And what about *C*s, that ultimate insult, a-v-e-r-a-g-e, a grade only one of Amy's English colleagues with elbow patches would give to a James Joyce because he didn't want to be caught flunking a genius or rewarding just a wannabe. And what about *F*s? To an Albert Einstein or even Johnnie Von Neumann, well, your guess is about as good as G's.

So G considered his options. He knew well enough that to stay in finite numbers or hunt for big primes, he had to work mainly within a university, and that meant having to teach at least some, which he didn't want to do ever again. There were a few companies around that had room for research, maybe 3M, IT&T, or GE, but that number was smaller than a shoe size, a number he associated with most of his DE students' IQs. In spite of his MIT degree, he knew that because he had deliberately stayed out of its network, his chances here were slim to none. So on the night that he left without a resignation notice to WSU-O, an institution that required him to sign a loyalty oath before he could receive his first paycheck, Ge threw everything from his apartment that he wanted to keep into his white canvas-topped Scout.

On his third trip to the trash container, his arms full of life's *things* that most of us don't even need or notice but carry from one place to another, his path crossed with one of his neighbor's, one of those Slavic men with a wide-chunked body, a man good with his hands. With his back to this approaching man and both hands useless, one hand on the container lid and the other lifting a heavy load of books, magazines and newspapers, G felt very vulnerable. He imagined him to be a USMC sergeant who's just survived three tours in Vietnam with a tattoo on his arm and a red bumper sticker with yellow *Semper Fidelis* on it on his pickup, or worse, a white man disguised as an Indian, a Chuck Connors sprayed with bole Armenia paint as Geronimo who'd just walked off a Hollywood set armed with a Winchester 94, its trigger guard altered, the 30-30 locked and loaded and ready to boogie with this gook of a G in front of an apartment dumpster in Oshkosh, Wisconsin, Heartland, U.S.A.

"You're that guy at the college aren't you," he said. Here it comes, reconnaissance, objective acquired and targeted, you'll never hear the bullet that takes you out.

G quickly spun around, but instead this man said, "I completely support what you're doing up there," his tone of voice gentle and caring, his right hand extended. "And I want to thank you," he continued, looking G in the eye.

G dropped the magazines and newspapers and books for the handshake and felt moved and weakened. With both of them bent over picking up his *things*, G muttered a weak *thank-you*. From this moment until he returned to his apartment, G was too shaken to remember anything else when he stopped by Amy's later to say goodbye.

"And he looked just like that man who tried to pick a fight with me at Howard Johnson's," G continued. "What made the difference, damn it?"

For a moment G felt he had made a mistake in quitting teaching, that maybe he had been too impatient with these people, some of whom are struggling with that same impatience. But it was too little, not enough to alter the bell curve, not enough to change the parabola downloaded from a basic nonlinear equation, only a wild and woolly unstable orbit that skips around and never settles down on the same spot.

Before G left, they discussed his options. He definitely did not want to become a statistician where there's plenty of work in insurance and banking. He didn't want to get into game theory and the maze of prisoners' dilemma and work for the CIA; or experiment with complex formulas and gargantuan computational work for NASA; or do spook work and encrypt mathematical formulas for coding or security contingencies for the expanding NSA in Maryland, mindful that the theoretical Alan Turing's 1939 move to Britain's Government Code and Cipher School had sacrificed a brilliant career, which G had already done when he flipped off Oshkosh, even if brilliancy had been in his stars. In his interest in fractal excursions and spatial designs, he was tempted to develop mathematical models for predicting and tracking the migration of leaking biochemical contaminants—aka nuclear waste, nerve gas—that was beginning to plague the Department of Defense, but he was also suspicious that such models would be used for the exact opposite purpose, and besides, he wasn't sure he could pass the necessary security clearance. And besides, he's not going to be just another apolitical mathematician, another motherfucker Chang, no way, not after what he's learned in the last three months.

Then G drove away, the lights of Oshkosh diminishing in the Scout's rearview mirror, first south, of course, then west, then east, then west again, finally east from Chicago, knowing that a PhD in finite numbers with his interests and concerns would have more options east of the Mississippi River unless he could land a job at the RAND Corp in California, a very low percentage, as every mathematician wants a job there. He left behind him a heartland where conservatism was viewed as the essence of strength and spirit of individualism. There were thousands of similar little places in it, isolated and insulated, places with no real connection to any other thing in life or to each other or the rest of the country, except that they all sing the same national anthem on fall Friday nights before the high school football game.

By the time he reached Lake Forest on the slower, old Highway 41, G knew he was headed for Pittsburgh to surprise his cousin Ted who'd just returned from flying a Cessna O-1 Bird Dog in a war that didn't exist in Laos.

18. BEST TEA IN CHINA

Ge and cousin Fei were discussing teas. The new No. 7 express from Beijing had arrived on a crystal clear morning, and when the sun came out it did not feel like winter at all. But *Whoa!* you say, *wait a minute here,* interrupting this otherwise seamless narrative. *The No. 7 express from Beijing to Chengdu did not even exist until Hong Kong was handed back to China in 1997. Ge took the train in 1968, so you said, several times, on page 16, page 47 and page 59, you blockhead of an author.*

So you're not taking a nap and you're reading carefully. Good. Excellent. But it still doesn't change the fact that Ge took a fast train from Beijing to Chengdu, a 32-hour-27-minute ride, if you must know exactly, and it was comfortable. Only foreigners like you Americans complain about train travel in China. And it still doesn't change the fact that Ge's cousin Fei met her at the platform, since arrivals and departures of every kind are almost always on time or ahead of time in China, especially departures. And having tea together in Fei's apartment on this crystal clear December morning that didn't feel like winter at all when the sun came out can't be changed, just as the fact that you're reading these words can't be altered either, not a word of it.

You might say drinking tea and talking politics is all that the

Chinese intellectuals ever do, their favorite pastime, maybe their only pastime besides looking for another job.

"And where do you think the best teas in China are grown?" asked Fei, pouring some more hot water into their cups from the thermos.

"I don't really know, but what I heard as a student in Beijing would put the green from Zhejiang, black from Fujian, and most from Hainan Island."

"Not so. Those are all on the coast. What do they know about growing tea? They only know how to export it. You've been in Beijing too long. The best is grown right here on the hillsides, green, black, jasmine, you name it. Come over here," Fei gestures, taking Ge to the window and pointing in the direction of the hills to the northeast. "See there, in the distance, above the Gold Star computer billboard, we'll take a bus out there tomorrow and you can see for yourself."

Ge wanted to know about the reports of Red Guard activity in Chengdu.

"It wasn't that bad, the eastern press has a way of exaggerating everything that happens out here. They only tore down the old palace that was already decrepit, and it's already been replaced by the Exhibition Hall, with Mao on the outside and those Russians Marx, Engels, Lenin and Stalin on the inside. But you know," Fei lowered her voice into a whisper and looked at the door, "there's talk that those portraits of the Russians should be taken down. You'll see, the showcase on Renmin Donglu."

After a pause, Fei resumed her narrative of Chengdu's modern history in a normal tone of voice. "When this city was the last stronghold of Chiang Kai-shek's KMT before he bolted for Taiwan, it was a lot worse, their massive destruction of our buildings, arbitrary confiscation of property and treasures, and the execution of everyone who dared to look defiant."

"Yes, I remember my father telling me that your province is very liberal and has a long history of resistance against the Mongol and Japanese oppressors, unlike the Changchun I've just come from."

"My second uncle? I've never met him, but my father has shown me some photographs of when they were in primary school. I couldn't tell which was my father and which yours. But you know what," and here Fei lowered her voice and looked to the door again, "I heard that they're talking about petitioning the NPC to give us back our two years wrongfully lost because our government could not control the Cultural Revolution."

"What? That's crazy."

"Shhhhh," Fei brought a finger to her lips.

"And which two years," Ge whispered, "When I was one and two? My last two years at Qinghua? And what about my teenage years—I'd gladly give up any two of those tortuous years. Then would that make me twenty four now, hah, hah?"

"It's just talk I've heard."

It bothered Ge that cousin Fei would not admit her own ideas but rather assign them to an anonymous source, and that she did not have a sense of humor. Ge missed Tang Li, her directness, her laughter, qualities she thought essential to a woman in keeping her spirit strong and vibrant while pursuing a professional career in an arena dominated by the male specie that would give them the occasional deferential look only when they were within the child-bearing age. Tang Li had no patience for these women who give in, and once described them as *shadows in the wind.*

"Well cousin Ge, we must start looking around for a new teaching job for you. Perhaps Sichuan University or Chengdu University of Science and Technology, they both have good math departments. This is a talented province and we have made great contributions to our nation's progress, including Deng Xiaoping and Zhao Ziyang. You can distinguish yourself in math!"

There was silence as Ge looked away, realizing that she had neglected to tell her cousin she had quit teaching, forever. Furthermore, Fei's xenophobic exuberant cheerleading was beginning to be most irritating.

"That's not what I'm looking for," Ge managed to say, despising herself for adopting her cousin's circuitous and trivial mannerisms that had nothing to do with life. "I plan on finding something with the government, maybe in irrigation or energy production, oil, coal, I'll find something."

"But your fancy Qinghua degree, you should be doing something more important."

There was another moment of silence, until cousin Fei said,

"You are welcome to stay here as long as you need."

But Ge already knew her need was fast diminishing, cousin or no cousin.

19. PLUTONIUM

It was right after spring planting, US President Richard Nixon's Bamboo Curtain-renting visit, and word started appearing in Chengdu streets heralding Sichuan's own Deng Xiaoping's return to Beijing and power as the vice premier of the State Council. But mostly it was the surprising early light of one spring morning suggesting innumerable promises that made Ge decide to ask for a couple of days off from her work in the engineering department of the powerful Yangtze Valley Planning Office.

"And what will you be doing," her supervisor Zhang asked, checking the posters around Ge's workspace one more time, to see if she'd added any new numbers to her primes chart with the last dozen entered in pencil to 3,021,377 and dated. A gentle man who always came to work in a white shirt, sweater and tie, he was also a mathematician and close to retirement.

"I thought I'd go visit some of the temples at Dujiangyan," Ge answered, one of her hands brushing her hair that she has let grow last winter.

"I didn't know you were religious." Zhang's eyes strayed to the other posters around Ge's computer monitor, a dated periodic table, a computer-generated graphics showing a basic spinel twin from a octahedral crystal's surface twinning, a panda bear in ink whose likeness was beginning to appear everywhere in Chengdu in every imaginable form from ashtrays to stuffed toys to cigarette and toilet paper brands, and a sun-faded *National Geographic* photograph of the American Grand Coulee dam.

"I'm not; I just want to get up to the mountains."

Zhang smiled. "Why don't you combine some work with your rest? Check out the old irrigation project while you're there? It's still functioning as good as it was more than 2,000 years ago. It might give you some ideas for your siltation modeling. And I'll send a car and driver with you."

"That sounds good, but I like to go alone, without a timetable. I like traveling alone." Ge noticed that Zhang has on his dark red tie. "It's not that far," she continued, returning his smile, "and the bus is reliable. But *xie, xie.*"

"Watch the pickpockets. I hear it's getting worse—they even have schools that teach modern techniques, advanced seminars in daylight, solo contacts for their best students." Zhang paused, then added, "Ah, modernization everywhere, but some things don't change—we keep sucking on that old teat."

Ge smiled at his leaving, but in a moment he was back.

"The suspense is over," he announced. "Remember the young and very ambitious civil engineer Chang with the crew cut? He transferred here from Chongqing last September without an English name and started looking for one from day one?" They both rolled their eyes. "He wanted to find the most powerful English word for his name to help his career, so people won't forget him? Well, the waiting is over; Chang has found his English name. It's *Plutonium;* now we call him Plutonium Chang."

Mouth open and speechless, Ge looked over to the periodic table, Pu, at 94, and could not hold back her giggles, hand over mouth.

> *Plutonium, plutonium, plutonium*
> *The Americans found it in California*
> *Where they find everything first*
> *Fired in a Berkeley cyclotron*
> *More fissionable than U-235*
> *Its neutrons 3.4 X natural uranium*

Two years later the Russians found theirs
Wriggling at the barrel end
Of their stolen neutron accelerator
Now maybe everyone has one
Israel, South Africa, India, Pakistan too
But not the people who need it most
Ask Clyde Warrior, he knows
So mail in your reservation now
In Sichuan we call him Vanity Chang

In Chengdu that late-April afternoon—the *Perfect Metropolis,* the capital of Sichuan Province of liberals and rice farmers (a contradiction if there ever was one) and more than 4,000 dishes, 4,000 flavors, 4,000 peppers, the hotter the better, most of them not even touched by Irene Kuo in her Borzoi, Chinese cookbook or tested and tasted by her editor, Pittsburgh's Susie Arensberg and friend of Pia Lindstrom—Ge had misled her supervisor Zhang when she said she wanted to visit the temples at Dujiangyan. What she really wanted to do was spend a weekend at the developing Wolong Nature Reserve in the high elevations northwest of Chengdu, hiking in the mist, thinking about everything in life, wondering if she would see a giant panda bear, *ailuropoda melanoleuca,* before all one thousand of them were belled by the World Wildlife Foundation for fund-raising purposes, or auctioned off to die in foreign zoos in exchange for currency, or eaten by the subsistenc e, cookpot natives, or given as ambassadorial pairs, like Hsing Hsing, Ling Ling and Cute Cute, so far to Japan, the United States, the UK, France, Spain, Mexico and North Korea. (It was rumored that one American zoo offered one thousand Holsteins in exchange for such a pair.) Who held the gun, and what was the barrel pointed at, Ge thought, when she concluded that her own desire to see them in their natural habitat was another unnecessary intrusion into their lives. Then she decided that what she really wanted to do was to go into the mountains where she can see beyond the end of her street and past the grotesque, giant statue of Chairman Mao. That was it, and Qingcheng Shan rising up from the Dujiangyan project was not that far away, which was what she ended up telling Zhang.

20. WATER GATES

As soon as Ge got off the bus, she literally found herself in the middle of the three main water gates of the Dujiangyan project constructed more than twenty-two centuries ago during the Qing Dynasty. These gates controlled the distribution canals diverting a good portion of the fast-flowing Min River into a year-round, intricate irrigation network of succeedingly smaller and more complex system of canals, weirs and sluices that irrigated three million hectares of agricultural land. She could also see the Flying Sand Spillway at the head of these gates that prevented flooding in the late spring and summer months when the run-off from the steep Qingcheng Shan appeared ominous.

During the short but bumpy bus ride here from Chengdu's western terminal, Ge read the recent letter from Tang Li, which she was still clutching in her hand when she got off the bus. Ge had not been prepared by the letter's directness in its defiance of Changchun and the university. Translated, it even took a swipe at the entire province: *this irremediable province of incestuous subservience whose collective* Fuck me, Fuck me *willfully forgave and forgot the Japanese atrocities committed against their own in the name of science during the 1930s.* No more little nudges of resistance for Tang Li; no more, just cautious little whispers to trusted friends.

This was a letter that stood the odds of one-in-six that it'll be opened, read and monitored before it's re-sealed and delivered. She's trying to get out or get thrown out of Changchun, or worse. Ge had carefully scrutinized the letter, its folds and its envelope for signs of tampering, and remembered their agreed strategy of gluing the letter to the inside of the envelope aligned to matching dots on both surfaces. She'd held the envelope to the light but could not find a dot on either the letter or the envelope, in case Tang Li had remembered, which she had not, or hadn't cared if she was found out. Just maybe, Ge hoped, in the modernization tempo of their nation, the censors were not interested in tracking anyone in literature—why censor it when no one read poetry anymore except in classes, and there with great disdain. Ge was more concerned for Tang Li's growing bitterness, a potential anger that could fatten and alienate friends and family, and if left unchecked, would eventually culminate in intellectual and emotional isolation and impotence.

Ge carefully tucked the letter in the body side of her pack next to her money and ID papers, away from the pickpockets, and started walking towards the apex of the diversion canal above the water gates, determined to help her friend Tang Li get out of Changchun.

"Where are your papers," a stern looking man with a cigarette hanging out of his mouth asked when Ge approached the main gate of the control terminal.

Not one to spill her IDs to any uniformed guard loitering about such an entrance, Ge defied him with an equally stern look and walked right past him into the inner compound. She wasn't about to give him any authority over her.

"Hah, hah, I see you're not one to pay any attention to our under-worked guards gorging on the government's rice bowl."

Ge turned around to see an older man inside the gate who looked as if he'd spent his entire life maintaining this project. Then she looked past him to see if the guard had heard him, and he had, scowling one hard moment before abruptly turning away. The older man was smiling and appeared not to be threatened by any outsider, or insider.

"How many IDs do you have? Four? Five?"

Ge remained awed and speechless.

"Let's see now, your brown Work Permit with photo, black Resident Booklet with photo, red Travel Booklet with photo, green permit to make Foreign Exchange Currency transactions with strangers without photo. That's four. And if you're carrying a library card, that'll be five. Am I close?"

Bewildered, Ge could only listen to his man, but started reciting to herself in such moments or when she's unable to sleep as much as she can remember, 3.14159265358979 32384626433832795028, half expecting him to continue …84197169399375105820974944459… go figure.

"Sorry. I guessed who you are, no? That hotshot finite numbers Ge working with my friend Zhang at YVPO. He said you would probably pay us a visit. I am Weng, and I've been working this project for the last forty years, and my father before that and his father before him, a total of more than one hundred years. You're among friends."

"*Hotshot*," were the only words Ge could mutter.

"Zhang and I only use that phrase to describe someone we like."

Ge looked at Weng, and could see that he meant it. "I've been very careful about what I say at the office."

"Yes, but Zhang knows what you've been thinking, and he agrees, even if he hasn't said it. You've been asked to make projections of the siltation problem for the proposed Three Gorges Dam while they keep you away from similar calculations for the Gezhouba Dam that's going up only a few kilometers apart on the same river. That's too much to believe, but one can say that only when we're far from Beijing, or from Beijing's surrogates like Chengdu."

Then they were silent. A moment later they both shielded their eyes and looked westward toward the steep, forested mountains as if it might provide some clues to unraveling the conundrum of the two dams, one under construction, and one certain to be under construction before the decade's out.

"You know," Ge said, "they've not allowed me to visit the proposed dam site yet, even with Zhang's support."

"They're too busy with its politics and funding to worry about if it's going to be a good dam or a bad dam. Every day they're bringing in and courting foreign visitors from Siemens, the US Bureau of Reclamation, the US Army Corps of Engineers, the American Consulting Engineers Council, Bechtel Civil and Mineral, Coppers and Lybrand, Merrill Lynch Capital Markets, Morgan Bank, World Bank, Asian Development Bank, and other financiers and consortia from Sweden, Japan, England, France and Canada. They may as well move the United Nations from New York to Chongqing. They don't have time for you, or Zhang. Or me. No one has asked for my ideas about these two new high dams, and my family has been working this low dam here for more than 100 years. Not once. I should know something about siltation in Sichuan Province."

Weng started walking out of the compound towards the inlet chute from the Min, and Ge had to almost run to keep up with this old man. At the gate the guard pretended he was looking at a tree in the distant mountains or a fly in front of him, same thing, Ge thought, resolutely laying one metaphor on top of another.

"It's just vanity, nothing but vanity," Weng was muttering to himself. "Look here Ge," he stopped and said, making a huge arc around them with his hand with the missing finger. "Everywhere the embankment is low, no more than five meters, but the channels are deep. No siltation problem here."

Ge was paying more attention to the missing finger, and imagined Weng giving up part of his body in a gear-locking accident.

"And even here," he continued when they had reach the inlet. "This we call the Precious Bottle's Mouth."

Ge looked at the sturdy, movable locks controlling the Min's flow into the main diversion canal.

"We're only letting in about sixty percent now at low water, but beginning in a couple of weeks, we'll start decreasing it to about forty percent during the river's high water in July and August."

"What about the siltation pile up here at the entrance," Ge asked.

"A good question. Li Ping and his son Li the younger were brilliant engineers twenty-two centuries ago. See the sharp downstream tail of that island there we call *Diamond Island?*"

Weng used the same hand to point past the sandbar to the island in the middle of the river. "During high water, the extra flow that's not entering this canal is shunted at high speed back to the river through this spillway, and that periodic flushing is sufficient to keep the entrance siltation free. It's never clogged up yet."

"And that's all, through all these years?"

"Not quite. As long as we pay attention to occasionally clearing out the canals and replacing the parts on the water gates, it could go for another 2000 years. During some periods of our difficult history, there'd been occasional lapses, but the damage has never been irreversible."

"Ah, master Weng, are you talking in metaphors now, hah, hah," Ge giggled.

"A river master talking metaphor, especially in Sichuan, you've got to be crazy. Everything here is literal, believe me, but I know you know that."

The sun had set below Qingcheng Shan, and the draft from the water was cool enough for the two of them to turn around and head back to the terminal compound. Ge walked step by step with Weng, and by the time they had reached the gate now guard-less but open, she'd decided that she'd go back to Chengdu that night and not waste any time tomorrow visiting the temples and their vast gods and their universe as she had planned. She had found a caring person in addition to what she had been looking for in going up there. In a grave moment there, high in the hills between the river and the mountains, she made a promise to herself that she will not allow her siltation work to be counterposed with lies, self-indulgence or vanity, determined that the rest did not matter, did not really matter at all.

At her departure, not another word was said. The dusk was rising fast and it was too dark for Ge to see Weng's eyes, but she could sense his nod, and it was warm and patient.

21. BIRD DOG

Out of there and into the theater of American trash talk of the 60s and early 70s. This is where you'll wish the author had thrown his pen into the fire and avoided this cock-and-bull story, unless of course you dig it because you had lived that time and talked the talk yourself. Not *dialogue*, but *talk*. This was the age of the hyperbole, the narcissistic show off, the drama and language of protest in an era of awakening political, gender and racial consciousness. This was language bout and poetry slam rolled into the same joint. Yeah, yeah, you're tired of this voice, its maniacal tempo annoys the hell out of you, *Let's get on with it* (I can hear you), but you gotta remember, this was the 60s and early 70s. And we got this guy G who'd barely survived Oshkosh and all of its deceit and conceit and political trash talk walking up to the front door of his cousin Ted's parents' house in Pittsburgh's Shady Side, the cousin who'd just come back from flying the same old Cessna O-1 Bird Dog for two years in a war that didn't exist in Laos. No siree, not if the collective Washington from A to Z, from Agnew to Ziegler, didn't admit or deny it, or the Pentagon or the State Department or the White House, and for that matter, or Johnson or Nixon or Nixon again, or the three Ms—McNamara and Magruder and Mitchell—or the three Hs—Helms and

Halderman and Haig—or the three Rs—Regan and Rostow and Rusk—interspersed with Kissinger and Ehrlichman and Dowd and Colson and Westmoreland and Daley, if they all didn't admit or deny it, then it most likely did exist. Without affirming or denying the existence or non-existence of a war in Laos, these men thought that our inquiry had been terminated, but we knew better.

It certainly had not terminated G's inquiry when he walked up the familiar five front porch steps of Westminster Place's last corner house of his father's brother, whose son had just returned from non-uniformed service in Southeast Asia, 1965–68.

Ted was waiting at the doorway, his dark hair getting long, a bushy mustache shading a smile. The two of them looked at each other a full moment before a tight hug.

"How long's it been," Ted asked. But before G could answer, Ted looked up the street and added another question, "What's that odd-looking rig you're driving?"

G followed his look. "It's a Scout, International Harvester you know, halved its V-8 truck engine for it. About as old as the last time we saw each other, what, five, six years ago, your graduation?"

On the way into the house, Ted said, "Yeah, good thing you called last night. I was going to check out my financial package at the university, but I got that done this morning. How'd you remember my dad's unlisted number from six years ago?"

"How can I forget MAin 1-1914! But what about your journalism degree?"

"G," Ted turned around. "G, you know how the war's being reported. Those reporters are either liars or lazy and sucking on feeds from press releases, same thing. Or worse. They line up twice a day at the trough in Saigon; I've seen them, once in the morning and once in the afternoon every day. They don't fucking know what they're reporting and don't care to know that they're just passing on lies. I want to know something about a subject; I want to know something about what I'm writing about, its background, its damn context, its implications. Trouble is, probably nobody'll give me a job if I wrote like that. You want something to drink, water, pop, beer?"

"Water'll be great," G answered and settled deep into the

indestructible, comfortable, large re-upholstered couch that the two of them had tried to destroy with their wrestling some twenty years ago. And it was the same couch that Ted's sister Kinka and her date made out in on some weekend nights, Ted and G spying on some heavy pawing and panting and French-kissing and erotic fumbling for the first time up close, and Kinka successfully resisting any un-doing of her clothes, no un-snapping, no un-zipping, no un-buttoning, no belt undone, nothing exposed, Kinka wasn't that kind of girl, she didn't go to Mount Mercy.

When Ted returned with the glasses of iced water, G asked him about Vietnam, the question that had kept him awake along the many Interstate and Turnpike miles.

"Well G," Ted began, as he sat down opposite him, the two of them returned facing each other once again as cousins and friends after incarnations in two other lifetimes. "I went in in 1963 because I wanted the pilot training, before the country knew we were in a war and had been for at least a decade. I flew, not the B-52s or the Phantoms—that's SAC and Navy and Marines—although my flight training started in them until they strapped us into the cheaper Lockheed Shooting Stars. I should've known what was happening right then. First Fairchild in Washington, then the Snake School in the Philippines.

"Because I wanted to be up there flying the newest high-tech planes, I volunteered. Before I knew it, I found myself in the Steve Canyon Program, would you believe they called it that? There in Udorn, Thailand, and later in Long Tieng, sheepdipped …"

"*Sheepdipped?*"

"Without a uniform and without dog tags and without a personnel file, as if we didn't exist, in a war that didn't exist. There we were, flight air controllers flying old Army Cessna O-1 Bird Dogs that had no armor or self-sealing fuel tanks, loaded down making sixty knots at 500 feet on a good day, each with a small, white pill of lethal shellfish toxin in case we were downed, compliments of the CIA.

"Our job was to interpret the daily changing Rules of Engagement, no pagodas, no civilians, no field hospitals, no schools, not even North Vietnamese MiGs on the ground until it was airborne and showing hostile intentions. We were tested on them every month. Go up, identify the targets with our 7x50s, call in the air strikes, swoop down and dust them with phosphorus smoke, then hang around and guess the bomb damage assessment. Sometimes we go up trolling, flying real slow to see if we can draw some ground fire before we dust it as a target. We did this in the *other* theater, Laos, Thailand, and Cambodia, this war that didn't exist."

There was silence, during which G started counting a new sequence to himself, *0, 1, 1, 2, 3, 5, 8, 13, 21, 34, 55, 89, 144, 233.* He stopped at 233, cleared his throat and asked, "How d'you feel about it?"

"What d'you mean," Ted shot back.

"I mean, there you were, somewhere between silk and cyanide, the airborne CIA, weren't you?"

"That's calling it. But most of us were pretty careful with our targets. Living there in Long Tieng with the Meo, the women with their beautiful headdresses of highly colored sashes. Most of the time we could tell who was who from the air at fifty miles an hour, but sometimes it wasn't that easy in any struggle for one's indigenous sovereignty, as these people were doing. And when we weren't sure, most of us just didn't make the target call. There was selective resistance, like those SAC drivers who dumped their load in Haiphong Harbor or Tonkin Gulf even rather than keep on bombing the same rice fields or worse, populated civilian areas, and some Marine flyers too."

There was another moment of silence as G tried to understand what his cousin was telling him. "Ted," he finally said, "Ted, I don't know how else to ask this."

"I know what's coming. We shouldn't be there in the first place, and I was part of it, and you're right. Short of going to prison, I was stuck."

"You mean to tell me Ted, that you killed people just to stay out of prison? That's incredible!"

Ted looked away, squinting his eyes toward the windows. "G, that's pretty easy for you to say." Then he looked directly at his cousin. "You who got your 2-F college deferment and kept on getting it through four years of grad school after your BS degree until you were too old. You have no fucking idea if you'd have done anything different."

G was shocked by the truth in Ted's comment. He remembered hearing that opposing positions on this war had separated countless families, but he was determined that it wasn't going to happen with his cousin, their birthdays two months apart, the star centerfielder with the rocket arm on the same team in Little League, then Babe Ruth, then Legion ball, the trips together to Philadelphia and Cleveland and once to Litchfield, Connecticut, to pick up a White Farm's copper beech sapling for their front yard. They were together at Forbes Field in 1960 screaming and jumping up and down as Bill Mazeroski's drive sailed past them at eye level before clearing the leftfield fencing to the side of the scoreboard for the winning run in the bottom of the last inning of the World Series game seven against the Yankees, screaming not only because they were loyal Pirates fans, but because they loathed the Yankees, especially Mickey Mantle and Roger Maris who also watched the same ball disappear over the fence into the beautiful red and yellow fall foliage of western Pennsylvania.

After a long silence, G said to his cousin, "You're absolutely right, and I apologize, I'm very sorry." Then he added, "But you sound as if you're against the war now."

"Thanks—I knew you'd come through. Strange to hear you talk like this. I wasn't going to say it until it was necessary, but I remember you going to all the debutante dances, hey, Lester Lanin and his beanies, Myer Davis, Griffith Williams. Boy, talk about sucking it up to the group that stands to benefit most from this war—they were welcoming Cuban refugees before we were out of grade school, sugar tycoons and bankers. But you know, this war isn't over yet. Just before I came back there was talk that Nixon's about to bomb Cambodia openly, that his press agent Walt Rostow is actually picking the bomb targets."

"With everything that's leaking out, how can they continue with this insane vanity that's destroying at least four countries over there?"

"I don't know, but I'm writing something for *Ramparts*, and most of the returning vets I know are actively opposing the war, VFW or no VFW. And Laos—that country is so beautiful, it should be turned into a park, all of it."

"And you, what was it like for you personally? I mean, your father's Chinese, but your mother's Norwegian with that impossible-to-pronounce name, *Cherste*, that no more than two persons in Pittsburgh can pronounce."

"At Long Tieng there was no problem, everyone did their job, except once in a while at the beginning I got some looks from the Meo men, but that stopped soon enough. At Fairchild's survival school there were some whispers, and once when I heard someone in the showers ask *How the fuck can I tell one slopehead from another?* loud enough I just wanted to storm in there and kick his teeth in. Like some of them didn't want to see that service .45 in my shoulder holster, some misplaced icon. Like I should have been shouldering an AK47 or a Punji stick instead.

"The town of Spokane near the base was worse — that domestic violence capital of the US — not even my damn uniform made any difference — those crackers had been using the word *breed* for more than a century. I was just another variation to them. You know G, this may seem odd, but I probably felt more pity and shame for them than they did, like they're still living in the last century?"

"Yeah, I know what you mean," G said, finishing the last of his iced water. "You should've been in Wisconsin. Damn, that place was strange, an odd mixture of HUAC's Joseph McCarthys and active resistance at both Madison and Oshkosh. Oshkosh, by gosh! It's one thing to protest in San Francisco or Cambridge or New York where you have some kind of community, but in Oshkosh, that's another thing entirely. You're on your own, man; there's nothing behind you, not one damn thing."

"You didn't mention Chicago, G."

"Well, that's another story entirely. Another first for them — Daley's goon squad wearing the American flag as their shoulder patch! I bet within the year every cop, sheriff's deputy, highway patrolman, civilian security guard, Turnpike toll collector and maybe even the Texas Rangers, FBI, ATF, INS, US Marshalls and campus cop will be wearing that flag. Militarization creeping up on us Ted, everywhere, that's what it is, that *brown-shirt* thing."

"Hey that's good. Think I'll use it in my article."

"Help yourself."

Ted took a deep breath and looked at G. "I'm exhausted by this, and hungry. What about going around the corner to that new place for a bite, the Balcony Cafe on Walnut?"

"Sounds great."

On their way out Ted asked, "What're you going to do with your fancy MIT degree?"

"You already know I've quit teaching permanently. I have a couple of leads at Westinghouse."

"You're welcome to stay here as long as you need. We have plenty of room here."

"Thanks. I'll take you up on it, at least until I find something. Westinghouse, they do everything from irons to jet engines."

They stopped to admire the copper beech in the front yard that towered over them in all its fullness, even above G's outstretched left arm.

"It's good to have you back," Ted said, "and it's good to be back together."

Rounding the corner, G just had to ask, "What about the Pirates for next year?"

"I dunno. There's talk they're going to trade Maury Wills. That'll be a mistake. They're still looking for a shortstop. Freddie Patek just can't do it."

"Maybe I should try out for shortstop, no?"

"You're kidding me. With your aim? You can't even hit a target ten feet away, hah, hah. They'll go back to Gene Alley."

"Then third base, if Wills is leaving?"

Ted stopped as they approached the end of Westminster Place. He turned to G and said, "G, G, goddamn it, with your arm at third base? Sanguillen just doesn't have the legs to keep on covering your throws to first. Forget it will you? You can't ever, EVER hit what you're aiming at with your goddamned arm! No way, not in a million years!"

22. HARMONIC TREMORS

It was right before the Pirates' spring training camp in Bradenton, Florida. G had been with Westinghouse for almost four years now, tucked away on a sidehill between the Monongahela and the Allegheny, doing "applied mathematical calculations" at the Science and Technology Center, for the folks that design and build—vector and matrix analysis in convergence runs for mobile wireless telecommunications networks, some high power matrix algebra work for jet engine cooling systems, and once playing with Fibonacci numbers and continued fraction expansion for EE's commercial lighting division, plus some sub-contracting assignments, like DE translations of vibrations and automated braking systems for Union Switch & Signal. Custom made to order at competitive prices, civilian, military, or industrial.

G was still playing with those numbers even though their applications for solving multi-purpose sports stadiums' lighting problems for baseball and football stadiums had been turned in several weeks before Nixon's historic visit to Beijing in February. He had always been fascinated with their possibilities: 0, 1, 2, 3, 5, 8, 13, 21, 34, 55, 89, 144, 233. Add the Lucas series to it: 1, 3, 4, 7, 11, 18, 29, 47, 76, 123, 199, 322.

And then the emerging Stolarsky sequence of positive numbers left out of the Fibonacci series: 4, 6, 7, 9, 10, 11, 12, 14. He's also playing with the idea of taking part of his vacation and flying down to McKechnie Field in Florida for a week with the Pirates' training camp.

"Knock, knock," a voice interrupted G's fantasy. Suddenly he's inside the office, the crew cut, C.Y. Lee who'd just transferred to OR's engineering section a couple of months ago, in probably the same white shirt and tie. "Are you still working on regression analysis?"

He'd been asking that same fucking question every time he'd seen G lately, as if it's funny, as if he knew anything about math or G's work. G didn't like him, not from day one, but CY has been tenacious in pursuing G's friendship. Was it because CY's degree was also from MIT, or that he was also Chinese, as G suspected was the answer. The reduction of life to such simple identity equations was beyond G's understanding or sympathy. Goddamn, he's from Taiwan, for crissakes. Next he'll be talking *brotherhood* and *motherland*, these little harmonic tremors that never register on anyone's Richter scale.

G turned away from his computer monitor, and sure enough, CY's staring at him or his monitor, all four eyes riveted, his leather-cased Lietz slide rule sticking out of his shirt pocket along with the colored pens, maybe the only engineer left in North America who's still carrying a slide rule. "No, just looking up prices of airline tickets to St. Petersburg," G said, pushing himself away from his desk.

"Oh, me too. I was looking for tickets to Denver and Seattle, you know?"

And that was another thing that annoyed G about CY, adding *you know* to every other sentence. But for some cautious reason G was patient, and asked instead, "You're going to those places west of the Mississippi?"

"Yes, we're consulting on nuclear waste disposal at both Rocky Flats and Hanford, you know?"

"I thought Hanford was DuPont's turf?"

"What's *turf*," CY asked, looking hurt.

"You know, *territory, property, owning it all*," and oh God, he's saying *you know* now, in CY's presence, because of CY's damn presence, who's looking around G's workspace with the eyes of a souvenir collector taking an inventory of his assets.

"Yes, but with the last of their nine nuclear production reactors scheduled to shut down in 1988, it'll leave 750,000 gallons of high level radioactive waste. Unstable iodine-129 that'll be around for more than a million years."

"One million years, wow! The new industry, nuclear waste disposal. They're probably wondering what language or sign to use on the toxic containers, so they won't be opened by some idiot archaeologist or developer a million years from now."

Noticing CY staring at the things around his console and feeling vulnerable and protective, G got up.

"I gotta get a drink," he said, and walked out to the water fountain in the hallway outside his office, CY slowly trailing behind him.

After taking a short sip, he turned to CY, making sure he had followed him. "Ah, someone making money in the cosmetic cleanup of the sacrifice zone ..."

"*Sacrifice zone?*"

"The West, the American West as the nation's sacrifice zone. First dig it up, chop it down, fish it out, kill it. Then 150 curries of airborne radioactive particles every day for twenty years. Now everything that glows, ship it to Idaho."

"But Hanford is not in Idaho; it's in Washington," CY protested.

G just stared at him.

"And Rocky Flats is in Colorado."

G continued staring at him.

"That vast area is the least populated area of America."

G started laughing.

"What's funny G, what's wrong?"

"CY," G finally said. "CY, my man, you've been in this country less than a year on a green card and you're defending our policies. We don't have to agree on everything here, it's not like ..." Here G almost leapfrogged the plot involving CY to the reader. Very untimely. We'll all have to wait and follow the narrative through, one word at a time.

"But what about this company that pays your salary?"

"Not even here, CY, not even here," G said, and walked over to the elevators, afraid that CY would follow him back to his office.

CY continued with his *buts*, claiming that it's not just the West, but the East had done the exact same thing too a century earlier, and especially here in Pittsburgh where it took a massive cleanup effort to change it. "They call it the Renaissance, you know?"

G didn't have the patience to continue and he wanted to go back to his office alone. "Let's talk about this another time. I have to finish some work on a deadline."

"Okay. It's Friday, and some of us are getting together for a drink after work at New York, New York. Why don't you join us? Isn't it near where you live, Shadyside?"

"Yeah, if I get the work finished."

Back at his console, G's curiosity about CY's motives was preempted by thoughts of taking a short vacation. There was the wedding invitation from Alix Houston, the other good student he had in DE at Oshkosh. He could go see Amy at her new teaching job at Colorado. Or he could go to the Pirates' training camp in Florida and try out for short—Freddie Patek's been traded, Gene Alley batted lower than .230 last season, and even less for Cuba's Jackie Hernandez brought in last year to help out at short, .206? G can do a lot better than that. Age? Not too old at thirty, younger than both Alley and Hernandez. And besides, weren't the Pirates famous for bringing in older rookies, like the 41-year-old pitcher Diomedes Olivo in 1960, born in 1919, for crisssakes. A forty-one year old pitcher who ended the season with a 2.79 ERA, and two years later a five and one record for them! And fielding? Great range, both left and right. Speed? The 9.7 in the 100 at the Drake Relays still there.

So at tryouts G'll bring his own bat, and the pitcher won't be some prick who'll throw him low and away curves. He'll return the three strikes he gets, first a 300 feet line drive, then a 350, then 400. Ten guys in a heat, he'll come in first in his race ahead of everyone else by so much that he'll be noticed. The coaches'll start making notes in their clipboards. Then every grounder hit to him that he can touch will be gloved and disappear into his throwing hand, wrist already cocked, and fired to first, belt high, faster than 100 miles an hour, the showoff arm trying to force two outs on the same batter, and it'll sail and keep on sailing into the fifteenth row bleachers above first at McKechnie Field in Bradenton, Florida.

23. SEDIMENTATION

I've never understood it. Once in a while
I look around and I see things familiar
and I think I will die here. It's my country then.
(James Welch, *The Death of Jim Loney*)

The Yangtze River, the Yangtse, the Yangzi, and now the Changjiang, the Long River. Like all major rivers that provide life for the country, so does the Yangtze for China, especially the agricultural Sichuan Province. And like all rivers, it provides an annual potential disaster in its flooding depending on the winter's snowpack or torrential summer storms. Its headwaters flow from the foot of the roof of the world, melting snow from the Tanggula Mountains of the Tibet-Qinghai Plateau, and it meanders a tormented 6,300 kilometers east across China until it's flushed into the East China Sea at Shanghai.

Like most rivers that can be both a blessing and a disaster, the Yangtze had its nests of residents who believed in its magical powers. Zhang had told Ge such a story coming from a low-lying village annually visited by the Floodwater Deity. Every year at the same time, all the villagers would escape with everything valuable they can carry, haul, pull or push, while the river surged threateningly above its waterline and mapped its way through the village. Every year after the floodwater subsided, sometimes in a week, sometimes in a month, the villagers would return with more things than they had left with and begin cleaning and rebuilding. At one point in the village's history, there was talk of trapping the Floodwater Deity with a net made of every string in the village, casting it across the river at the height of the flood and anchoring one end to the giant banyan at the bend in the river just above the village. The villagers believed that if they could only trap the Floodwater Deity, haul it out of the muddy water and let it dry in the air and sunlight for three consecutive days, then the floods would cease forever and never again devastate the village. But there was no one in the village committed to this belief enough to organize the effort, farmers being what they are, and not everyone was willing to sacrifice every piece of thread, rope, string, yarn, twine or lint for something they were not entirely sure about—they knew they would at least eventually use that last piece of saved string, if only to tie some duck's legs together for the market. In the end someone muttered that it was a good thing they had not killed the Floodwater Deity, since the end of the floods would also have meant the end of rain, the end of crops, and the end of their way of life. So then as with before, there has been the annual flood every spring, a certainty they can count on running away from and later would return to, the exact same spot in the landscape to rebuild whatever the river had taken away, before they put in their new crops, before the river would take away again next year. It had never occurred to them to move elsewhere from the river's flood plain. *Like the river, China goes on forever. If you stop the river, you'll stop China.*

Then came the dams. For flood control, for hydroelectric power, for irrigation, and for transportation. But there are problems with dams, and the foremost is sedimentation, what the river leaves behind to thwart man's vanity and greed. For low dams, regular maintenance dredging can be effective most of the time. Then there's salinization, which has always been a collateral threat as in India, Mesopotamia, Sumeria, or Egypt's Aswan or North America's Anasazis. For the high dam, silting and sedimentation are unusually dangerous to a dam's longevity. Unless it's breached before its usefulness is terminated, the disaster caused by the water held back in its reservoirs can be more destructive than the 1954 flood with a flow rate of more than 76,100 cubic meters per second on the Yangtze when more than thirty thousand people were drowned.

Sedimentation is not going to go away, Ge thought; as long as there are rivers, there's going to be sedimentation. *If you stop sedimentation, you'll stop China*, Ge giggled. *Like sedimentation, China goes on forever.* And the Three Gorges Project she was working on for the YVPO was asking for a dam height between 150 and 185 meters. As a mathematician, she was mandated to study the sedimentation potential. That's what one did in China, she thought, a woman with a PhD in finite numbers from Qinghua, with everyone in the world looking on, from members of at least ten state ministries in China to the CCP Central Committee in Beijing, from the bankers sitting on the boards of directors of the World Bank, the Asian Development Bank, and Morgan Bank, to those investors controlling Coopers and Lybrand, Merrill Lynch, Guy Atkinson, Bechtel, Morrison-Knudsen and Stone and Webster, while the sales representatives from companies specializing in automatic distribution systems, transmission systems, generators and turbines such as General Electric, Mitsubishi, Mystere, Électricité de France and Siemens salivated as they waited in the hallways outside for their contracts.

So far with Zhang's support, Ge's managed to visit the proposed dam site twice, once to visit with a team of Chengdu University of Science and Technology's hydrologists taking measurements that provide the data for her work. And on another trip she spent two days with and a group of archaeologists busily taking preliminary inventory of the 1,300 known cultural sites along the 500 square kilometers of the river bank that will be totally submerged with a 150-meter high dam, sites that date back to the pre-Han period. These were good and important visits for her, especially watching the hydrologists at work. She was confident that the numbers they were sending her as raw data were reliable, that they had not been politicized, yet. She was however having a problem with their feudal methodology borrowed from the US Army Corps of Engineers.

She was also aware of the transportation problem, how two Nanjing bridges stood in the way of ocean-going vessels headed for Chongqing. Then there's the endangered Yangtze River dolphin, the *baiji*, the river horse, *Lipotes vexillifer*. With fewer than 300 of them left, environmentalists have predicted their disappearance with the construction of the high dam. Geologists have expressed equal concern with the size of the backup reservoir: the weight from the 700-kilometer lake will surely create significant pressure on the earth's crust to trigger massive earthquakes. Some military leaders have worried about the vulnerability of the dam's generation of hydroelectric power equivalent to seventeen nuclear powered plants reduced to a single target that can be easily targeted from India, Pakistan or even a silo in Kazachskaja. Public health officials have talked about the jeopardy posed by water-borne diseases finding a home in the large lake and the reduction of the quality of drinking water. Ge was however moved more by the painful displacement of the peoples that the government had already begun to relocate to large municipal areas where they arrive homeless, many of them ethnic minorities — Miao, Yao, Lolo, Yi — in whose name the dam's new irrigation capability is supposed to feed. The published number was 40,000, but Zhang had said that close to a million will be more realistic. Ge was convinced that the government's claim that these DPs will not be homeless was a lie. She also suspected that as they find their desperate way as exploited day laborers and service workers into the urban centers of Chongqing, Kunming and Chengdu, and even as far away as Beijing, Wuhan, Guangzhou and Shanghai, they will remain there homeless for more than just one generation — they will become the permanent underclass, while the dam-irrigated agricultural land from which they were evicted becomes monocultural to feed the urban rich in Beijing and Shanghai, and for export.

For now, sedimentation was all Ge could work on, and she was still determined to do it right. For four years now, she had been convinced that something could be done to lighten the Yangtze's heavy sediment load. Since the river's width nor its depth could be altered, the only solution left for sediment control has to come from reducing it at its point of origin through massive soil conservation programs. Over its history China has periodically mandated such efforts, sometimes with success, but mostly failures the farther the program's location from the government. But since she suspected that the government's huge bureaucracy wasn't about to change for the TGP, she had no choice but to continue doing her isolated and outdated work.

As a newcomer, she learned very quickly that sediment was divided into the wash load, the suspended load and the bed load, and that the morphology of the river determined its transport. The measurement numbers sent up by the hydrologists indicated site, time, and amount. What Ge hoped to accomplish was determine the relationship between discharge, sediment transport, sediment size and river slope. Such a model was extremely involved and laborious, and could hide errors of a few 100%, if not by a factor of ten. The data the hydrologists supplied her were inadequate to make her predictions reliable. She constructed logarithmic scales of total bed material transport from bed load plus suspended bed material load in tons per day per meter width, to determine the uniformity of the bed material as the function of discharge and river slope—but what about the grain size? 0.1 or 1.0? She wasn't getting that number.

She concluded in her first year that a river with the width of 300 meters and a slope of 0.0001 produced a discharge of 60,000 m^3/second with a uniform bed material of 0.25 mm. Yield for the entire river bed, 1,600 tons per day. But where are the coefficients if the grain size were mixed? On top of that, all these predictions provide a function of only one single discharge—actual rivers have fluctuating discharges. What was she doing here?

She wanted to be responsible for her work when she knew that the judicial structure in China had never held decision makers responsible. She'd scoured the archives at Sichuan University's library and learned that the successors of the world's periodic hydraulic agriculture had built colossal political and social structures at the sacrifice of many lives through the creation of despotism, absolute power without benevolence. Certainly China's first emperor Chin Shih was no exception—after he consolidated the monster Great Wall, he ordered 700,000 workers to construct his palace and tomb. She also read that once such hydraulic despotic hegemony is established, the society tended to establish central control, and economic and resource planning become one-sided. Ahah, she concluded, the so-called traditional family structure of China owed its *pater* authority to the backing of the despotic state and its laws. *Disobedience to the father was punished by the government. Wait till I tell Tang Li this. She'll flip.*

Ge was also plagued by the incongruity between the necessity of sediment removal and flood storage, since they occur simultaneously. What'll her final report tell Zhang, that there will be a sedimentation problem, and the only solution appears to be massive annual dredging, into the indefinite future?

At night her worst nightmares when the wolves are out showed a Yangtze all plugged-up by its crumbling banks, the arable lands submerged all the way back to Tibet, and downstream, downstream at Shanghai, the sea level rising and rising. Astonished? No, not even a monkey in sight in their province. Ge will worry about this some more when she wakes up in the morning all worn down.

24. THE KMT

On another Friday evening after work a year later, G's footing it down Kentucky Avenue to the new jazz club New York, New York to meet the group from R&D. The Pirates had started this season with Gene Alley at short, and G had been thinking about trading in his drafty canvas-topped white Scout. He's worried about its age, another cycle of new tires, wiper blades, battery, starter, fuel pump and light bulbs, the dipstick's constant rubbing against the radiator hose, and the manual lockout hubs for engaging the four-wheel drive. Not that he'd used the 4x4 much since moving to western Pennsylvania, but the temperature had been below zero the couple of times he had needed it. Maybe a more conventional car this time? An Oldsmobile or Buick for G, hah, hah.

When he first took walks after moving into his apartment, he had memorized the streets one after another, Denniston, Shady, Emerson, College, Maryland, all twelve or thirteen blocks to Giovanni's or the Balcony on Walnut where he'd meet Ted on some weekend night. But now several years later these names have altogether disappeared, replaced by a sense of place, the white bricked house with the rocker on its front porch, that Mr. Hodges walking the twin terriers around the block at least twice a day, one black, the other white, the green house with the two gingkoes in the front yard, that garage with one out-of-school teenager succeeding another working on their '55 green and white Chevy coupe, and distinct noises that come out of houses, the domestic yelling, a third position screech of a violin, a blaring radio or TV, and from that house on the corner, the smell of garlic and anise and sometimes marijuana. Give him another year and he'll be able to tell you exactly where he's at blindfolded, in white, Middle America.

CY was waving at him from the OR group by the table near the window, his slide rule still sticking out of his pocket, ready just in case he needed it to make some square root or cosine or tangent calculation for someone's ritual martini or Manhattan or the EEs' favorite, Rum and Coke, when everyone at the table can do it in their head in less time than it'll take for the Lietz to clear its leather holster.

When G got to the table, the EE Jeff looked at him and said, "If you and CY are going to talk politics, I'm leaving."

The others at the table agreed, including CY, but Heather held back. "You're going to talk baseball instead," she asked.

G looked at her, smiled and answered. "How can you ever talk baseball with these engineers who're all American League fans? That's not even real baseball. No bunting, no stealing, designated hitter, pitching specialists, no way is it baseball."

Napkins and olive pits were tossed until they settled on movies. By the time the waitress had taken their dinner orders, they were talking about the new Bruce Lee movie, *Return of the Dragon*.

"Great fight scenes, especially when Chuck Norris gets killed in the Roman Colosseum ..." Jeff said.

"But it's the same old plot," Heather interrupted. "There's nothing there but the same old, same old Chinese immigrant story of family loyalty, honor and revenge," she continued, looking at G, expecting some support.

"Hey," G said, "don't look at me Heather. Remember I'm not into movies? I haven't even seen *The Graduate* yet." Heather's description of family loyalty, honor and revenge stuck with him, a way of explaining Taiwan's and Hong Kong's fixation with the motherland, and for that matter Miami's too, something he'll have to check out with Amy later.

"Did you ever ask him why," Jeff asked, but decided to answer the question himself. "He thinks when something is liked by more than six persons, it can't be any good, a Bernie Shaw saying something like that way back. So when a movie is liked by almost everyone, like *The Graduate*, he thinks it's got to be some cheapo cultural commodity hijacked for the masses. Right, G?"

"Something like that, but it's not all that serious, just kidding. I wonder though, is this Chuck Norris going to take revenge on being killed in this movie by an Asian? I mean, he's white?"

"You're getting too serious G, picking everything apart. This is only entertainment," Jeff said. "It's only entertainment," he repeated.

"Yeah, maybe you're right."

And so, on into the evening until Heather had to leave, then a couple of the other EEs, then Jeff, until only CY and G were left. G felt CY staring at him again, the ever-watchful souvenir hunter looking for a collectible, or just maybe a Kuomintang agent trolling for a plumber, a Mossad Katsa with his hooks out looking for an asset to be dry-cleaned, curried, cultivated and fertilized.

With a few drinks behind him, G decided to bring it into the open. "All right CY, you can shut down your microwave antennae now. What's this all about? Why have you been staring at me and my work for more than a year? Out with it."

At first CY was hesitant and would not even look at G, but when he recognized this moment initiated by G as the exact one he had hoped he could set up himself, he decided to carry out his mission. "I'm an agent," he said. "I'm in this country to find out who's on our side and who's the enemy, you know? We send so many students here—we need to know the political map."

Annoyed by the *you know*, G wanted to know who's we, damn it.

"You know, the Chinese," CY answered, looking surprised.

"Which Chinese," G asked, becoming belligerent.

"The Chinese in Taiwan of course, and all the overseas Chinese, the diaspora Chinese, we're all the same. I'm surprised you didn't know which Chinese, G," CY stammered.

"Chinese my ass," G said, unable to check himself anymore.

CY looked away and asked G to lower his voice. "We're making a scene," he said in a whisper.

And the Chinese are not supposed to make a scene? Maybe CY hadn't been to enough Chinese restaurant kitchens in this country.

"Okay, okay, but Chinese my ass," G said, lowering his voice. "You Taiwan neo-Mandarins stopped being Chinese the moment Old Peanut Head Chiang Kai-shek and the Kuomintang left China in 1949. When he paddled across the Formosa Strait to Taiwan in his rowboat, the Chinese in him slipped from a noun to an adjective. Don't you dare confuse the KMT and its old Shanghai Green Gang hoodlums with the Chinese in front of me, you bozo slide ruler."

G stopped to order another drink from the waitress. CY was starting to look embarrassed. But G could also tell CY was mad as hell that he had totally mis-assessed his mark for fourteen months.

"Furthermore, you're not even Taiwanese, those that you tried to colonize or kill off, including twenty-nine thousand in the first week of your landing, a little trick you'd learned from the Japanese in 1937 Nanjing." Here G paused before continuing, "And the US Cavalry. You're dictators running a police state but call yourselves Taiwanese and raise the KMT flag! You're flying the wrong fucking flag you bozo."

G wanted to push a little more after his drink arrived. He'd had it with this pissant CY and his KMT. G had enough troubles of his own as a chink in white, Middle America that he didn't need this additional confusion and harassment. "You're not Chinese no matter how many times a week you and your father face Xiamen or Fuzhou and jack off. And don't give me this consanguinity crap. Like the French in Vietnam, Old Peanut Head wasn't using the free Land Lease weapons on the Japanese in WWII, he was saving them to use on his own people, so don't give me any of this brotherhood or motherland thick-blood crap. You haven't even been there."

"They weren't Chinese, they were Soviet-trained communists, traitors to the motherland and the spirit of Dr. Sun's revolution," CY interrupted.

"You're pathetic CY, the whole lot of you, and I'm not going to listen to the rest of your line," G said, but he was not quite ready to leave, not just yet. He'd remembered what Amy had told him on their weekly phone call last weekend, Amy and Joyce who kept their ears to the ground and learned everyone's secrets and passed them on to him, and he continued, "So the KMT is all pissed off by Nixon's visit to Beijing last year and the signing of the Shanghai Communiqué, getting kicked off the UN's Security Council and being replaced by Beijing, the ultimate insult and betrayal. And now its gang of all gangs, the gang from hell, the ever vigilant and always violent Iron Blood Patriots and its goon squad Ju Kwang go apeshit in the US checking out who's on whose side and murdering those without the right portfolio, huh? No wonder Hong Kong's making all these movies, like Taiwan, Heather's family loyalty, honor and revenge."

CY became ever alert at the mention of the Iron Blood Patriots and Ju Kwang. "So you know about us," he said. Then threateningly he added, taking his slide rule out of its leather case, "We'll see how much you know.

"We're on many campuses. Here in Pittsburgh we're at Carnegie Mellon, University of Pittsburgh, Duquesne, even nearby Slippery Rock. We keep files on all the Chinese, no matter what you say, students and professors, whatever passport they carry. We follow them into libraries and bookstores and find out what newspapers and books they read. We keep a record of what movies they go to, and who their friends are. Sometimes we use our own wiretaps and send our reports to both the FBI and the CIA in addition to our own agencies." CY interrupted himself to peer at an imaginary calculation he's working on his slide rule.

"Your J. Edgar Hoover relies on our surveillance for his reports on the subversive activities of your so-called Chinese Americans, and he has the full cooperation of both the INS and the IRS. The only American agency that has protested has been the Postal Service when the CIA demanded mail-opening privileges at their San Francisco terminal where all the mail to and from China goes through. And that went nowhere. We even initiate the shutting down of Asian studies departments on your campuses across the country. So G, you better watch your mouth before we turn you in as a commie, you know."

"You forgot to mention your cover organizations CY," G said, taking a moment to get all the names right. "Pacific Cultural Foundation, Asia and World Institute, Institute of International Relations, Sino-American Cultural and Economic Association, Chinese-American Association for Science and Technology, New England Association for Chinese Professionals, Chinese American Librarian Association and more, no?"

They stared at each other until CY smiled.

"How d'you know all this G," he asked. "I thought you were a mathematician with a passion for baseball and a white girlfriend in Colorado."

"Now you know more, and you don't know what to do with this new information. I'm going home, I've had enough," G said, and got up to leave. "See you at work."

"Maybe not," CY said, returning his Lietz to his pocket, "maybe not."

By the time G got to Kentucky Avenue, there were only a few houses that still had some lights on. G remembered at one time he had thought about going to China and seeing the birthplaces of his parents, and he had talked about it with Ted who was also interested. After the confrontation with CY this evening, G was beginning to wonder about the meaning of visiting a relative's birthplace decades of political and cultural cycles later. If any relatives could be found, what would he say to them when they have all gone their separate ways for close to a century? Ancestral roots, emotional roots, identity politics, little wisps of words disappearing into the cool, early May morning.

25. WOUNDED KNEE

The three of them were having a great time on the light PAT going downtown to the second of the Pirates' three-game weekend series against the visiting Mets, and you're spying on them, the maggot that you are, though without premeditation, or design, I think, though I suspect that from two rows back the more you read, the more you'll have to read.

"It's been years since I've seen a major league game," Amy declared, her Shreveport Louisiana accent lilting behind her tonsils just waiting to get her into trouble. The two black men standing in the aisle overheard her and looked at each other but said nothing.

G and Amy talked about driving up to see Wright's Fallingwater the next day, but Ted was going to be busy.

"That's easy for you to say, Amy," he said, "you're on spring break. I'm looking for a job and I need to get my résumé and portfolio ready by Monday. The drive alone to Fallingwater and back's a good two hours."

"Résumé?" Amy asked. "That's easy. I can help you; I teach a course in technical and professional writing, and sometimes I think that's all it's ever useful for, writing a résumé, I mean. We'll do it in less than 30 minutes!"

Amy explained that there are only two kinds of résumés in the world, regardless of the kind of job you're applying for. Downsized, the models are either 1) *The Dirty Dozen*, or 2) *The Magnificent Seven*.

"Think about it," she asked. "D'you want to appear to your future employer as John Cassavetes, Donald Sutherland, James Brown or, heh, heh, Telly Savalas as some information on a clipboard; or as Steve McQueen, James Coburn or Charles Bronson who had to demonstrate who they are?"

"James Brown," one of the men next to them asked. "Not me—they kill that sucker at the end of the movie. He dies in just about every movie he's in, damn opposite of that white boy, John Wayne. All but two, and that one 'cause they didn't want to change history."

"Which one was that," his friend asked.

"That'll be *The Alamo*. He even directed that one. The other's *Sands of Iwo Jima*. The only time he's killed in more than 200 movies, once by a Jap, and then by a Mex. Think about that message."

G wanted to agree, but he's easily exasperated by analogies, especially this crooked one about résumés. He nevertheless took the time to think about it. In *The Dirty Dozen*, your future employer Lee Marvin who'd set aside his service .45 just for this purpose, already has read your conventional résumé attached to his clipboard: he already knows everything there is to know about you, and in the case of Telly Savalas, much more than that. In *The Magnificent Seven* you have to prove who you are to the cigarillo-smoking Yul Brynner, the consummate professional. He doesn't even have any money to pay you—it's an honor just to work for this guy. Cool, but what does this mean about the résumé?

They're taking timeout at the T transfer downtown, and we just have to be patient for the answer.

Sure enough, Amy did not let us down. "So, Ted," she said after finding an empty seat on the shuttle to Three Rivers Stadium, "it's either the quantitative, conventional résumé, aka the new patient's intake history, the soldier's service file, the McDonald's restroom cleaning record; or the qualitative one that actually reveals who you are, what you're good at doing and what your potentials are, like the baseball scouting report, no?"

"Okay Amy," Ted said, "after the game why don't you check over my shoulder while I do it? Then we'll all go to Mill Run tomorrow in my car, since his Scout's not working. I'll throw something together for dinner."

They found their seats six rows up from third base where they could see into the Pirates' dugout.

"I miss number 19," G said quietly to himself, pensive.

"Miss who?" Amy asked, offering up her popcorn.

"Roberto Clemente," Ted answered. "You've heard what happened to him on that food-and-medicine relief flight last year."

"Oh yes," Amy said, but her recognition was interrupted by the national anthem.

Having lived through the sixties and with the war still on, the three of them, especially Ted who had served and been sheep-dipped and flown a Bird Dog, the three of them could not feel this sense of national unity in flag raising. They stood up, but instead lowered their eyes and heads until the last home of the brave faded into the fans' cheering. G wanted to see what players like Stargell and Oliver and Sanguillen were doing during the anthem, but he didn't raise his head to peep, an orthodoxy that had been drilled into him by the sisters at a Catholic grade school.

The game was a disappointment. In third place, half a game behind the Mets, the Pirates needed this one, even if it's only the second weekend in May, having lost the night before four to three. Driving back from Lake Erie, Amy and G heard that game on KDKA, including the Pirate pitchers hitting three Mets players, Cleon Jones by Dock Ellis in the fifth and Rusty Staub and Jerry Grote by Ramon Hernandez in the seventh. And in this game too, Duffy Dyer got on base on a HBP. And with Willie Mays on the DL — playing out his career back in New York where it started more than twenty years ago — along with John Milner, no wonder G thought he saw Mets manager Yogi Berra pitching batting practice when they first got into the stadium.

Tom Seaver had his stuff this night, nearly a no-hitter except for Pirates starting pitcher Bob Moose's single in the third and Willie Stargell's triple in the seventh, which G had argued would have been an inside-the-park home run if only Stargell would lose fifty pounds. Halfway through the game Ted looked at the program and saw that Seaver had entered this game with a 1.61 ERA, which he thought should make up for several of the Mets' DLs. Halfway through the game G started scribbling in the program, playing with an algebraic equation for describing Seaver's curve ball: $F_m = K_\omega VC_v [1 + 0.5 \times (V/C_v) \times (dc_v/dV)]$ with a 3.4" Sagitta and a deflection of at least 14".

"Provided no one fucked with the 60'6" distance from the pitcher's rubber to the plate last night," Ted added, looking over G's shoulder.

And so it was, the Mets ahead 1-0 until Jim Rooker came in relief in the eighth, and with three consecutive singles by Jones, Staub and Kranepool, it was all over, two more runs, and Dave Guisti giving up another three in the ninth, a 6-0, two-hit, shutout for Tom Seaver. G noted to himself that Gene Alley had a fielding error in the sixth and marked it on his scorecard, E-6 and circled it in red ink, next to his equation for Seaver's curveball.

"Good thing we didn't get tickets to tomorrow's game—this series could be a sweep for the Mets," G said as the three of them left the stadium.

"G, don't be so negative," Amy said in her best vixenish, Scarlett O'Hara imitation.

Ted heard Amy and looked over to G. G didn't know whether to laugh or pretend Amy hadn't said anything, but his eyes pleaded to his cousin, Please don't say anything.

For Ted, throwing something together for dinner tonight meant pizza takeout, so he'll have more time to work on his résumé on his typewriter, with Amy's help. G's watching the evening news. Tonight it took the news from South Dakota nearly a week to reach the eastern media, about the same span of time it took for the news of Custer's defeat at the Battle of Big Horn to reach New York almost a century ago. It followed Eric Sevareid's reportage of the Supreme Court for CBS and the slowdown of peace negotiations in Vietnam. The five-second visual only showed Russell Means and Dennis Banks and a few others walking away from their siege of Wounded Knee, and the narrative described it as the orderly end to a series of inner tribal disputes that started back in February. But G knew the rest of the footage that was not aired: they were being herded for processing by the FBI and federal marshals at Roadblock-1, over one-hundred-fifty men, women and children surrounded by armed federal troops, sheriffs' deputies, state troopers, BIA police, ranchers and vigilantes, waiting to be interrogated one by one, fingerprinted, photographed, some arrested, but everyone to be hunted and hounded by the law for the rest of their lives.

"Amy, Ted, look, quick," G started to say, but they were already tuned in to this story.

"G, didn't you teach there for a year," Ted asked, "right after your MIT degree?"

"You mean South Dakota," Amy answered, G's official biographer in such moments. "He was in Brookings. Pine Ridge or Wounded Knee's clear across the other side of the state, closer to Nebraska and Wyoming."

"You've been there Amy? I thought you two met in Oshkosh."

"She keeps her ear to the ground," G said, looking at Amy.

"Not me; you must be thinking about someone else," Amy corrected G. "But you know," she said, slipping into her Shreveport Louisiana voice, "I do keep my ear to the stove, like Constance Towers and Althea Gibson in *The Horse Soldiers*, you seen it?"

"Then between the two of you, what really happened there," Ted asked.

"And this is what I've heard," Amy started. "On February 14, several Lakota grandmothers led a protest against the fascist tribal leader Dickie Wilson, you know, the one who uses the John Birch training film *Anarchy U.S.A.* to convince people he's on the right side and doing good for his people? They just wanted the feds to come in and conduct a fair impeachment hearing and monitor new elections. Thwarted, they asked for help from the American Indian Movement, AIM, who came in, and added to the original list by asking Senators Mondale, Humphrey, Fulbright, Kennedy, and Abourezk to convene Senate hearings on Indian treaty rights land claims."

"This is South Dakota, Ted, you've got to remember that," G warned. "When I was teaching there, the Indian population outside of prison was nine to one, but inside, it was close to one to nine. The big annual event was Lawrence Welk going home every summer and taping a show from the Corn Palace in Mitchell, for crissakes."

Amy and G cleared a spot on the dining room table and proceeded to map out a chronology of recent events on some typing paper:

November/1969 Occupation of California's Alcatraz Island
August/1970 Fish-In in Washington with the Nisqually, Puyallup and Muckleshoot
April/1971 Occupation of Minneapolis' Fort Snelling Naval Base
August/1971 Occupation of Milwaukee's Coast Guard Base
February/1972 Raymond Yellow Thunder demonstration at South Dakota's Rapid City and later Mount Rushmore
November/1972 Occupation of BIA Headquarters in Washington, D.C.

"Wow," Ted took a full breath. "Look at this list, it's a 20th-century Manifest Destiny from west to east."

"It's a reverse wagon train," G contributed.

"They call it *The Trail of Broken Treaties*," Amy informed them, her ear to the ground, or stove, or from scanning the distant smoke signals trying to waft their way east across the Mississippi River.

Between Amy and G and Ted's newspapers, they pieced together what those 150 almost-unarmed men, women and children faced in their occupation of Wounded Knee. Colonels Jack Potter of the Sixth Army and Volney Warner of the 82nd Airborne deployed 17 APCs, 130,000 rounds of M-16 NATO (7.62 or .223) ammunition, 41,000 rounds of M-1 ammunition, 24,000 flares, 12 M-79 grenade launchers, 600 cases of C-S gas, 100 rounds of M-40 high explosives, as well as helicopters and maybe all the F-4 Phantom jets that were not assigned to Vietnam or flight training. And that's not counting what the federal, regional, state and local law officers and vigilantes were equipped with.

Ted leaned back in his chair and locked his fingers behind his head. "Why is this happening," he asked, slowly. "It can't be revenge for Custer's defeat—the Seventh Cavalry made sure of that at Wounded Knee. And why now, this year?"

Amy and G looked at each other, and then at Ted, and then at the enveloping silence. Amy got up and left the room, out the back door to light a cigarette on the porch, leaving G absolutely speechless.

There are moments of silence that should be respected, a time when the past, present and future jam together into something that needs to be sorted out. Leave out the talk that exacerbates the strain of conversation; just chill out and take some time to figure out what is the real topography on your own.

"The Lakotas gave up land for the Fort Randall Dam," G said, moments later. "The Confederated Colvilles for the Grand Coulee Dam, the Umatillas and Warm Springs and Yakamas surrendered Celilo Falls for the John Day and the Dalles Dams ..."

"What G's leading up to is this list," Amy interrupted G, back from her cigarette. "With Exxon, Shell, BP and ARCO in Alaska in 1971, now it's Union Carbide, Gulf Oil, Phillips Uranium, Kerr-McGee ..."

"Kerr-McGee," Ted interrupted Amy and finished the list for her. "DuPont, Dow, Boeing, FMC, Michigan State, Cardinal Spellman. It's the same fucking thing that's in Vietnam isn't it; we've just replaced the French. Greed and power, or power and greed, whichever. We're still doing it; we've been doing it for five hundred years—the corporate and government war against our neighbors and against ourselves."

In that night of startling exchanges, the three of them had forgotten how to clap their hands. Until there is genuine reconciliation, it'll be doubtful what their clapping will mean the next time someone hits a home run or sings the national anthem.

1990

26. BRIDGE

> *"But play, you must…*
> *A tune upon the blue guitar*
> *Of things exactly as they are."*
> *(…)*
> *Ourselves in the tune as if in space,*
> *Yet nothing changed, except the place…*
> *(…)*
> *And that's life then: things as they are,*
> *This buzzing of the blue guitar.*
> (Wallace Stevens, "The Man with the Blue Guitar")

Tang Li and Ge were thinking about cooling off from the summer humidity by taking a walk across the Jialing Bridge whose construction was completed only two months before the Red Guards found their way to Chongqing. A small unit of PLA soldiers out in public drill had just stepped onto the bridge from the bus station side on the opposite shore. Ge reached out and tugged on Tang Li's coat sleeve.

"What's wrong, Ge?" Tang Li asked, looking across the bridge at the marching soldiers and hearing an order that brought the detail to a complete stop. "Didn't Mao say that the PLA was the people's friend?"

"Tang Li, tsch, tsch, you don't have to be so sarcastic, I was only thinking about the harmonic waves in their chest cavities."

"What are you talking about? Didn't you once say that a white horse is never just a white horse in China? Give me a translation—what are you talking about?"

They could hear the snapping of another order, and the detail proceeded to walk out of step across the bridge.

"There, see, it's okay now, we can go across now, they seem to know what they are doing." Ge explained that when a group of soldiers are crossing a bridge, they have to break step to avoid the harmonic transfer of their breathing that would damage the bridge's pylons. "A lateral vibration created by their harmonious synchronicity," she added, visualizing its equation

$$f - \frac{w}{2\pi} - \frac{1}{2\pi} \sqrt{\frac{k}{m}}$$

"Ge, tell me you are not speaking in metaphors," Tang Li insisted again, looking straight at Ge.

It was summer, and even while the water level on both the Jialing and Yangtze that converge at the Chaotiamen Dock at the northeastern tip of the Chongqing peninsula was beginning to recede, it looked to be another exceptionally hot and humid day, a smokestack, like Wuhan, Nanjing and Shanghai downriver. After more than ten years of trying to leave Changchun for another teaching position, Tang Li finally found an opening in Shanghai's Fudan University. On her move south she took a detour to visit China's West. She had also wanted to see the Long River, the Yangtze, and the Three Gorges before the next dam changed everything.

Ge was not speaking in metaphors. In fact they'd both agreed after last June's events at Tiananmen[2], no one in China'll ever use them again. They saw what happened as the result of a homily gone sour, a defective parable that boomeranged, a lesson learned from a faulty fable, that the students and others had in fact been killed by friendly metaphor. Tang Li even thought that with Tiananmen[2], the stupid little students in Beijing had naively and gloriously acted out the party propaganda movies they were required to view in grade school, except just this time maybe they mistook the party leaders for the KMT or the Japanese Imperial Army, or foreign aggressor, whatever enemy that rose to their memory's foreground and that couldn't have been much, since their schoolbooks were deficient in truth. From now on, the country's going to fly Deng Xiaoping's *To Be Rich Is Glorious* banner. To hell with metaphors! Metaphors are for revolutions that fail!

They'd also discussed Mao's dictum for the social and political function of art, which he'd passed down the mountains in Yanan in May 1942. Art can never swerve from party ideology he'd declared, and overnight, everyone's tongue in the country rolled with metaphors once more. And if not? One Ming emperor in the 1500s chopped a dissident to pieces and furthermore executed 900 of his extended family, neighbors, fellow students, teachers and friends, just as a warning.

"But beware," Ge had giggled on the train. "Stopping up the mouths of the people is a lot more dangerous than stopping up a river. When a river is blocked and then breaks through, many people are bound to be hurt. It is the same with the people."

But that was a joke last night; Ge was not speaking in metaphors, at least not since she left Changchun. "No, that's not a metaphor," she finally said.

Tang Li apologized, two intellectuals quarreling on this bridge in Chongqing, the rill of words. By now the PLA detail had reached them, their green uniforms stained black with sweat, several with shirttails hanging out. Ge couldn't help but wonder who'd be the most ready to die for these half-baked ideas they'd been throwing around, the intellectual or the soldier. Maybe the best thing would be to throw them over the side and let them sink into the river. But then, would they transform into a wash load, suspended load or bed load, and would she have to construct another logarithmic scale to determine their impact on sedimentation? Ge was aware that her logic had been strange lately, and she'd wondered if her work on the dam had been the source.

In their hotel room that night after supper, Tang Li opened her suitcase and produced a sheaf of papers carefully wrapped in soft, red tissue paper, tied with a piece of string. She laid it carefully on the side table between them and untied the string.

"It may be impossible for me to make use of what I know about this country. It burns within me, and it stays within me, right here," she said slowly, her right fist touching her chest. "I can't say what I know today, because that information can hurt a lot of people I'm connected to. And tomorrow, tomorrow no one will be interested, and besides, it won't be true anymore."

She looked over at Ge, her dear friend. "I can't say it in my classes, even when I know it's the best thing they can learn from me, in some classes the only thing. But Xie said I must bring these papers and tell you."

Ge was glad that at last Tang Li had brought up his name. They had been together nearly three days now, and the omission could have meant only one thing. But Ge also knew that even as Tang Li's best friend, she couldn't ask, because they'd both learned very early in life on their own separate paths that if you're Chinese and you cannot handle loss, you won't survive in the 20th century, regardless of the internal pain and isolation that'll accumulate from your decision to go at it alone. This moment was not the time to ask about her husband Xie, however.

"These were letters never sent, five years of them, from Xie's bridge partner in prison, but they gave them back to him when he was released last month, a gesture to appease Amnesty International after Tiananmen[2] last year."

With both hands, Ge accepted the pack of letters offered by Tang Li, maybe as many as a hundred, or more. Tang Li explained that Xie's bridge partner was a Liu Yong, a musician who'd liked foreign music groups too much, especially Talking Heads and Sting. He'd written a song with the lines, *First we eat our conscience/ Then we shit ideology* and sang them in a Beijing bistro that was already being watched. He was arrested, then disappeared, and no one found out what happened to him until his release on national evening news, locked up in Beijing's Prison Number 2, aka New Capital Engineering Works that manufactured radiators and machine parts.

"When he was released, he said a lot on TV," Tang Li related. "'This is a surprise to me,' he said. 'I did not know when I woke up this morning that I was to be released. But it seems all of you knew. Ah, how little purpose the story of one's life is, how insignificant when it is compared to what others want to claim from this story.' He also said, 'I did not know who the prisoners in the other cells were. They made no noise and were so quiet, I thought they were intellectuals.' Then still on camera, he bowed his head onto the table and started sobbing opening, and soon farting uncontrollably."

For five years, he'd kept himself together by remembering every spot on every card in every hand of bridge that he'd ever played, its auction and its eventual play. It hadn't mattered to him that he did not know if his letters survived the censors and were sent to his partner Xie. Now, Ge was here looking at them.

"Maybe the guards were suspicious of the numbers, that they were coded messages, or maybe they knew exactly what they were, a record of bridge deals, a bourgeois, Western card game, a staple form of entertainment among the diplomatic circle and some missionaries in pre-revolutionary China, whatever."

"Yes, but didn't Sichuan's own Deng Xiaoping, didn't he also play bridge," Ge asked.

"And a lot, that Mr. Panda Man. And he was punished for it, especially when he ordered state trains to transport his bridge team around the country to tournaments. But the real trouble for him started when his partner Hu Yaobang, who was a much better player carrying Deng, so Xie tells me, when Hu suggested in the mid-1980s that the Hands should leave Tibet and let them rule themselves.

"When Liu reached Changchun he gave the packet of letters to Xie, the same packet you're looking at.

"Strange thing, though. Xie asked him to go down to the Chess Academy for the Tuesday duplicate bridge game they used to play every week, but Liu declined, saying he'd completely forgotten how to play the game, and Xie said he'd meant it."

Ge started leafing through the packet slowly. One by one she carefully lifted each sheet and read them in its small, penciled script, until she got used to Liu's handwriting, even though she did not know the first thing about the game, except that it was played with a deck of 52 cards.

"You know, Tang Li," she said in a whisper. "Maybe China always needs to have a prisoner."

#308

```
                        ♠ AT75
                        ♥ KQ53
                        ♦ AQ2
                        ♣ 73

♠ QJ43                                        ♠ ---
♥ T2                                          ♥ J9876
♦ 764                                         ♦ T98
♣ QJT4                                        ♣ 98652

                        ♠ K9862
                        ♥ A4
                        ♦ KJ53
                        ♣ AK
```

NS—Vul

S	W	N	E
1♠	P	3♥	P
4♣	P	4♦	P
4♥	P	6♠	P
P	P		

Opening lead: ♣-Q from W, S wins with ♣-A
Trick 2:   ♠-2 from S, N wins with ♠-5
Trick 3:   ♠-A from N, wins
Trick 4:   ♠-7 from N, S wins with ♠-K
Trick 5:   ♠-6 from S, E wins with ♠-Q
Declarer claims.

#332

```
                        ♠ QJT94
                        ♥ JT9
                        ♦ 5
                        ♣ 7643

♠ 73                                          ♠ 5
♥ KQ84                                        ♥ 632
♦ KT6                                         ♦ QJ9872
♣ AKQJ                                        ♣ T98
```

♠ AK862
♥ A75
♦ A43
♣ 52

Both sides — Vul

S	W	N	E
1♠	D	3♠	P
4♠	P	P	P

Opening lead: ♣-K from W, wins
Trick 2:   ♣-Q from W, wins
Trick 3:   ♣-J from W, S wins with ♠-2
Trick 4:   ♠-A from S, wins
Trick 5:   ♠-K from S, wins
Trick 6:   ♦-A from S, wins
Trick 7:   ♦-3 from S, N wins with ♠-T
Trick 8:   ♣-7 from N, S wins with ♠-6
Trick 9:   ♦-4 from S, N wins with ♠-J
Trick 10:   ♥-J from N, W wins with ♥-Q
West is endplayed and declarer claims

Holding hands then, Ge and Tang Li studied these two letters toward the bottom of the packet, then they looked outside their room's window into an early full moon, two moons, the one above and the one below reflected in the shimmering Yangtze. They tucked the sides of the letters together, folded the red tissue paper over the top, and their four hands carefully retied the memory of these letters, even though neither of them understood the game.

27. WEATHERMEN

On that early morning before Amy had to fly back to Denver, they stayed in bed and took a good and frisky digression from this narrative. They talked about going into the living room and drawing the shades and playing on G's mother's big piano, the 1941 Steinway with the cast iron plate, its heart growing stronger with each note. They talked about slipping out in a nineteen-foot Corinthian on a musty, August evening and tacking the red Dacron sail to the left of her thigh. When the wind picked up, they sailed away in the endorphin flush, an even keel among the starboard bells.

Much later, after the champagne and orange juice and coffee, Amy's dejected by the thought of leaving and going back to teaching. "You're lucky; you found a way out G," she said.

But G wasn't so sure about that. While it's true he didn't have to pretend to work daily with the little pissant students that litter every DE class on every campus, he's beginning to see how his work at OR perpetuates the system that cultivates and promotes them, little enzymes with baseball hats waiting to be cloned and mass produced.

"Well, I'm not so sure about that," he said. "Unless one's teaching, it's almost impossible to do any significant math that won't be eventually compromised by the military. Or used for technological surveillance by industry or the government. For power, control and greed."

They recalled the 1973 summer trial of the Weathermen. Overshadowed by the Senate Watergate hearings, Bernardine Dohrn, Mark Rudd and William Ayers' asses were hauled into a Detroit court on the charge of plotting a campaign of wild terrorist acts against Kissinger, Nixon, the Pentagon, and every university laboratory that funneled its research to the military or Dow Chemical.

"Four months into the trial," Amy reminded the two of them, "the Justice Department dropped all charges it had spent three long years in building, surprising everyone in the media. They didn't know how to report the event and decided to ignore it and focus on Watergate instead."

But Amy knew, and now G knew. The gathered evidence had been illegal, results of secretive watch lists, black bag techniques, the Huston Plan carried out by a little known spook agency in a self-sustaining spook community—its own schools, medical facilities, sports arena, movie theaters, grocery stores, credit union, dry cleaners, massive computers, banks of microwave antennae and post office. On highway maps, it's designated Fort Meade, Maryland, this National Security Agency that has less Congressional oversight and more budget than the CIA. Rather than admit to the obstinate Federal District Court Judge Damon J. Keith that such incriminating evidence against the Weathermen had been illegally gathered through a wide-network of government, technological surveillance against its own citizens with the assistance of IT&T, Western Union and RCA, and reveal the existence of the NSA, the Justice Department was obliged to throw in the towel. It wasn't just the FBI or its KMT surrogate doing their little indiscreet wire tapping, but NSA's extreme measures of extensive electronic surveillance was focused on every citizen. It knew more about ourselves than we cared to. Do you know exactly what groceries you bought last week, item by item?

"You remember my friend Kathy at Oshkosh?"

How could G forget her low-cut, see-through fishnet top that kept him from a brawl at Howard Johnson's!

"Well, she wanted a child, and took a sabbatical to hide her pregnancy from her department. On her return, she stopped inviting friends over to her house, and hid the fact she was a mother, afraid that being a mother would hurt her academic career. Not wanting to risk anything, her husband does all the shopping. It's probably a good thing he's an engineer, otherwise he probably wouldn't put up with this charade. When they go away on holidays, they leave at night and come back at night. Their drapery is always closed, and they never let anyone into the house."

"Amy, Amy, stop it—you're making this up."

"Only a little, not much," she said and closed her eyes, leaning against the refrigerator. That's all she could say, holding the last words in her mouth before letting out a sigh.

At the airport concourse, Amy tucked a note into G's coat pocket when they hugged goodbye. When she called that night from Colorado, G still hadn't noticed the note. He found it later, along with his keys and some old wrappers. Amy had written *Don't you miss me? Remember to turn off the lights. XOXO Amy.*

Amy had once told G there's always someone in one's life who's constantly on the watch, turning off lights and every electrical appliance that's not in use, and then there's always someone who's leaving everything on. Now she's saying this same thing from Colorado, but G was not sure who was who at that moment.

28. PLAINTEXT

The shades to her workspace were drawn against the afternoon sun. Ge was sipping tea at her console, growing more troubled by the sedimentation computations she'd been crunching out the last several months. Modeled for a 150-meter dam, the same basic data had been recycled for a 160-meter dam, then for dams at increments of five meters until it reached 185 meters. She knew something was wrong here; she was not about to assume anything: she's a mathematician. Something's incomplete and dramatically wrong in making slight nudges in the equations and formulas to allow for each five-meter increase in the dam's height, when the entire methodology should be dramatically redesigned for a river being transformed from the lifeline of some ten provinces into their economic workhorse.

She'd thought about coming up with a radically different sort of computational program that would work out any arithmetic problem as long as she knew how to write down that equation. It seemed like a trick question and reminded her of a high school exam question: say Nanjing is 200 kilometers upriver from Shanghai (which it is not—some chaos people would say today it's closer to 400) and the Yangtze flows at 10 km/h and you're driving a riverboat that goes at 20 km/h. How long would it take to go from

a) Shanghai to Nanjing, and b) Nanjing back to Shanghai? At that time she thought only an idiot would be fooled by the 10 km/h speed of the river—the riverboat either traveled at 20 km/h, or it didn't. But the real trick, aha, was more complicated and involved the hydrodynamics of the river, the faster current in the middle channel and slower to the sides, over deep pools, and then those unpredictable bends that took generations to understand. The only reliable answer to the question would involve long hours of working out partial DEs and then computing them.

She thought this Three Gorges Dam was a gigantic experiment in vanity and greed, if it worked. What was meticulously measured now—bed load, suspended load, sediment load; during high velocity flow, medium velocity and low velocity; in the river's aggradation and its degradation—will be totally altered when the flow rate and depth of the Yangtze are changed by the completion of the dam's construction that will create a storage reservoir of some 600 kilometers long all the way back past Chongqing. Ge anticipated that a reservoir so huge will form a new, complex flow morphology and create unknown, shifting, three-dimensional density currents in distributing sediments—totally unlike the present river's characteristics that the hydrologists had been meticulously sampling and bottling and measuring in futility for longer than Ge's been with this project.

And what about the essential collateral studies? Were there other departments that she didn't know about within her agency now renamed the all-powerful Changjiang Water Resources Commission that were looking at the other environmental and human effects of the TGP? Her supervisor Zhang had mentioned that the Soviet-trained hydrologist, Premier Li Peng—possibly the most despised man in China, especially since Beijing's political spring of 1989—had already been promised the overall directorship of the CWRC, his golden retirement parachute. The answer to her questions seemed bleak. The dam project was going ahead, regardless of her analysis and recommendations. One way or another, the dam will be constructed, another monster tribute, like the Great Wall or the Grand Canal or the Pyramids or the Grand Coulee. And there will be mugs, postcards, icons on hats, ashtrays and every imaginable twinkle including DayGlo condoms that will be hawked and paraded from one tour office to another around the world without end.

Ge stared at the primes chart to the side of her monitor, her hands in her sweater pockets. Nothing had been added to the last entry 3,021,377 in years. With summer approaching, she reminded herself to cut her hair shorter. Her right hand felt a piece of paper in the pocket with her keys, and she took it out and unfolded it. *Don't you miss me? Remember to turn off the lights. XOX.* Ge read the message in English, but the last section of the message was missing. She searched for it in her pocket, but she could only feel her keys and a candy wrapper. How did this get in her pocket? And what was the message, especially the XOX? She looked in her dictionary but couldn't find any word starting with X and followed by an O. Then she substituted the other four vowels, one at a time, still coming up empty. Maybe it was in code, the first two sentences in plaintext and the fragment in cipher text? With only three letters in the cipher text, a standard substitution couldn't take more than a couple of minutes to work out, including a regressing transposition search for the repeated letter X, even when the message had been truncated. Less than a hundred tries, at the most. But what if the first part is the cipher text, and XOX the key?

After an hour, Ge lost patience with this game. In pencil, she wrote *Indecipherable, like the TGP* in English below the message and taped it to the top of her monitor before turning off everything at her workspace.

1994

29. CHUGWATER CREEK

> *We took out our heavy revolvers (all of*
> *a sudden there were revolvers in the dream)*
> *and joyfully killed the Gods.*
> (Jorge Luis Borges, "Ragnarok")

On his vacation, G was on I-25 northbound for Cheyenne a good half hour before dawn. Amy could not go with him on his first visit to the American West if you didn't count his year of teaching DE at South Dakota in 1967, the year of its champion baton-twirling Silver Twins. On deadline to Cambridge University Press for her book *Post-Structuralism and the Gendering of the Text: Stand by Your Man,* she had to stay in Boulder and finish out its indexing and final page proofing. At $59.95, that's "pretty good for rubbish," she'd said the night before, don't you think? To let him know he could count on her, she'd volunteered to keep an eye on her electronic mailbox twenty-four hours a day and provide stovepipe answers to questions arising of place and space west of the 100th Meridian; and to keep him company, she had given him a list of animals he could encounter along I-25 from Trinidad to Billings if he'd look close enough, a seven-page printout generated by a friend in Colorado's Wildlife Division.

At daybreak he pulled into a crowded truck stop outside Cheyenne for breakfast, and wondered if he was in the real West yet. "What'll you have, hon," asked a name-plated Shirl from the other side of the counter. Ham 'n eggs 'n hashbrowns, you said. Then the short-skirted waitress popped her gum and stared at G with her oranged face, her pen poised over the receipt pad. "What else, hon?" So this is that shorthand dialogue between genders in the West G had read in Owen Wister for this trip? Which came first, who copied whom? Questions that had an entire century to play themselves out until they had no more meaning then as now—it is believed.

So G settled for solace in the wildlife list, uncomfortably wedged between two men in flannel shirts and silver belt buckles the size of dinner plates who would not acknowledge his presence or each other's. The greenback cutthroat trout's not the only endangered species in this part of the country—a flaw in the naturalist's reliance on the use of computers, satellite imaging and remote sensors. Somewhere between the primes 337 and 347, the seven-paged Wildata Listing for Vertebrates in the Trinidad Latilong Block started with the tiger salamander, plains spadefoot, New Mexico spadefoot and included three toads, three frogs, four grebes, two geese, three teals, two widgeons, at least nine ducks and five hawks on the first page alone. By the time his breakfast order arrived, he'd ticked pencil marks next to the great blue heron, tundra swan, Canada goose, red-tailed hawk, mule deer and pronghorn as those most likely to be seen driving at 70 miles an hour.

G took the west frontage road at Exit 47 about thirty minutes out of Cheyenne. As he slowed down for the exit, tiny mottled beige flecks moved in the corner of his view, and he turned to see five pronghorns grazing by an oil drill—another pencil mark later. Cousin Ted had asked if he would take a photo of the Minuteman III silo Q11 at Chugwater Creek three and a half miles on County Road 244. "It's there, unguarded, part of the 90th Strategic Missile Wing out of Warren Air Force Base, but you probably wouldn't see it unless you were looking for it," he had said. Look for something resembling a small power substation with a few poles on a couple acres of concrete slab enclosed by cyclone fencing topped with barbed wire. G saw it coming over the top of a small hill. He stopped the car and got out his Nikon with the 200mm lens.

When he looked through the viewfinder, he could see a white Air Force van parked next to the stairway leading down to the underground bunker for the shift exchange of crews who looked as indifferent as office workers getting off and on a PAT in downtown Pittsburgh. Ted said these double-keyed officers are tireless and vigilant in front of their computers and monitors, ready to launch, in 31 seconds, their missile with three independent nuclear warheads, each 25 times more powerful than the U-235 Little Boy that destroyed Hiroshima. "But don't worry; you won't glow."

As G snapped the shutter on his FM2 the second time, he noticed another, larger herd of pronghorns, these bedded down on a winter-wheat-covered hillside a little half mile back of the silo, forming a tranquil, pastoral postcard then against the snow-capped mountains in the background and a sky of the deepest blue of blue over everything. Here, then, together, flora and fauna in the nuclear heartland of a West of mostly conservatives who simultaneously distrust and trust their government but can't get by without sucking on its teat even as they're continuing to be exploited, they're the first to be targeted in this national sacrifice zone, once more in the late twentieth century.

G was nervous as the two cars passed each other moments later on the narrow CR-244, as he should have been when you stop to think about it. The only chink in the state not with the university at Laramie must be a spy for the PLA, or an Oriental at least 1,200 miles from his kind on Interstate-5, in a rented Japanese car and a Japanese camera snapping pictures of an ICBM silo in Frontier Days Wyoming that had lobbied for these military installations. He was relieved when the Air Force van didn't even slow down and the driver waved at him, "Howdy, pard."

[About this time you're pointing out an editorial error, that Asians and Japanese in particular are not new to Wyoming. There was a whole city of them during WWII, fenced in with guard towers and machine guns, up there about twenty miles on a rail siding south of Cody, Heart Mountain, a stone's throw from the Wind River Reservation. In fact, at close to 11,000 it was the third largest city in the entire state, behind Cheyenne and Casper. You don't say. Yup. Up there then, in Harvard's Teddy Roosevelt's and his buddy Owen Wister's last outpost of civilization and the first outpost of frontier individualism and determinism and westward expanding Manifest Destiny, in 1943, 1944 and 1945, small clusters of Arapahoes and Shoshones and small clusters of Japanese Americans stood staring at each other in wonderment across a tiny strip of Wyoming State Highway 120 separating them, the Red Savages and the Yellow Peril eyeballing each other and wondering what the other was doing there. Yup. At this point I, the copy editor, must intrude and confess that I do not know which one of us has written this paragraph.]

So this was the West then, the West he twice started driving toward that evening in 1968 he left Oshkosh and teaching for good before he thought twice, no, thrice, and turned his Scout east for Pittsburgh instead. This was the West where the Indians are kept under permanent house arrest. This was the West that's become the national and global dump for toxic waste, the grids mapped for the testing, storage and siting of nuclear weapons and Motel 6s. This was the West where the systemic violence against Indians, women, children and animals has been the price paid for believing in the romance and allure of rugged individualism and self-reliance that was never true in the first place, or the last.

So that night in one of the two red-white-and-blue Billings Motel 6s across the street from each other that smelled of stale cigarette smoke, disinfectant and moldy alfalfa, G turned on the TV to the middle of a *Kung Fu* episode. For years he had secretly wanted to watch it, like *The Graduate*, to see for himself what it was like. Now was his big chance.

There's David Carradine playing Kwai Chang Caine somewhere in the West—it could have been Billings a century ago. He's a breed, plays a mean flute, little bubbles his emotional curve, talks real slow and deliberate, a minimalist, often in parables, travels light, and is real good at some kind of Shaolin martial arts. He's also wanted by the law of both China and the United States, but G couldn't tell why. Right now he's in a flashback getting a lesson from his master, played by Keye Luke. Oh my god, Master Po's blind. He says: But do not go with fear, Grasshopper. Fear is eternal darkness. Go instead with inner strength, for it is like a deep river into which all streams flow. It increases, always moving forward, and soon there is nothing that can stand in its way. I hear the water; I hear the birds.

G's falling asleep, but Kwai Chang Caine, he saves the horses, the children, the women, the whole damned town, but in the end he has to leave town, *Come back, Shane,* come back in a white Air Force van, to the home of the brave, ending the broadcast day.

30. THE LAST OUTPOST

China's premier Li Peng, the Soviet-trained hydrologist, was on a shopping spree in France and Germany this summer, anything he could get his hands on, on the Changjiang Water Resources Commission's Three Gorges Project credit. Industrial turbines, transmission systems, generators, automated electrical distribution systems, from Siemens, from Électricité de France, as well as subsidiary turbines from General Electric Canada. Like other decision makers in China before him, Li Peng will be rewarded if the TGP becomes a success, but will be exempt from responsibility and blame if the project fails.

But without power like the third-generation caretaker Weng of the Dujiangyan irrigation project north of Chengdu, the reverse will be true for our Ge, her agency will be located: she will be held responsible when her recommendations for eliminating sedimentation problems cause construction delays and cost overrides in the dam's budget; but her work will be ignored if it doesn't, unless unchecked sedimentation forecloses the dam before the projected completion date of 2016 when the generated hydroelectric power is expected to go online, in which case she will also be held responsible. Maybe the River Dragon will come during its construction stage and wipe out the cofferdam and then the entire project. Maybe the River Deity will come like it did in the form of an inland typhoon in the summer of 1975, or masked as flood-control measures on the Yangtze in 1954, when the indestructible Iron Dams of Banqiao and Shimantan both collapsed, causing close to 250,000 immediate deaths. But Ge knew it was a fantasy. Her immediate problem was the data that'd already emerged from the almost new, five-year-old Gezhouba Dam a few kilometers downstream on the same river, showing sedimentation had already usurped 44% of its reservoir's storage capacity.

So while Premier Li Peng spent a few days in Europe in the 1994 summer, Ge took an Air China flight from Chongqing direct to Hong Kong to get away from her work for a few days. And to see this *Pearl of the Orient* in its last days as the last British outpost, or was it fast becoming the first Chinese outpost? Exactly ten years after President Richard Nixon's visit to Beijing that normalized Sino-U.S. relations in 1972, Prime Minister Margaret Thatcher slipped into Beijing in 1982 and initiated bilateral discussions that would return Hong Kong, Kowloon and the New Territories to China on July 1, 1997, as indicated in the Joint Declaration signed two years later. Since then, Tang Li had written Ge from Shanghai, a giant clock had been set up in Beijing's Tiananmen[2], day and night counting down the seconds until the official handover ceremonies.

Tang Li had also advised Ge to be careful what shoes she wore in Hong Kong. *They'll be looking at your shoes to see who you are.* Her husband Xie who'd been to Hong Kong a few times in his year with a pharmaceutical in Japan, had added, *Don't wear anything that'll suggest you're Japanese.* And in a phone call just before she left, they'd both suggested that she use English and avoid using Mandarin on the streets whenever possible.

And that's what she did, pretending to be mute, carefully handing a written hotel destination to the cab driver at Kai Tak Airport, who kept on suspecting her in the rearview mirror all the way down to Tsimshatsui's YMCA. But at the registration desk, Ge was confronted by a rude woman who addressed her in Cantonese. When she looked up at Ge and could not understand her Mandarin, she wanted to say *You're not Chinese,* until she thought something's not accurate about that. Ge's passport and travel documents silenced any further remark from the clerk, who followed Ge's every movement in the lobby for the rest of the week with a look between suspicion and awe. Tall and traveling by herself, Ge was beginning to get very annoyed by the vast number of shorter Hong Kong people staring at her—never had she been so stared at in her life, not even when she was the only woman graduate student in finite numbers at Qinghua.

Ever since looking at those prison-survival bridge records Tang Li had shown her in Chongqing four years ago, Ge had wanted to know more about this game, and thought Hong Kong would be the place. Her visit to the four bookstores around the YMCA produced nothing on bridge, so she went back to them a second time looking for some fiction by Hong Kong writers. Much to her surprise and embarrassment, she could find multiple copies of Han Suyin's *Love is a Many Splendored Thing,* Richard Mason's *The World of Suzie Wong,* Somerset Maugham's *The Painted Veil,* Anthony Cooper's *The Sanctuary,* James Clavell's *Noble House,* but nothing by a Hong Kong writer, not even at the gift shop at the new Cultural Centre, or the huge Swindon's behind the Y, or the South China Morning Post Bookstore on Nathan Road or its popular outlet at the Star Ferry terminal. There were novels by D.H. Lawrence, Laurence Sterne, Jane Austen, Margaret Drabble, Anthony Trollope, Charles Dickens, Samuel Butler, Virginia Woolf, Joseph Conrad, Evelyn Waugh and Emily Bronte. Nor could she find a novel by a Chinese writer, Lu Xun, Wang Meng, Mao Tun, or Ding Ling, not even a copy of Cao Xueqin's *The Dream of the Red Chamber* in any of its multiple translations.

Ge concluded that for the last 175 years the people in Hong Kong have been kept in a cultural prison fenced-in by these books projecting an English homogeneity she suspected did not even exist today in London, Oxford or Cambridge. But since 1982, this last British outpost was beginning to look like the first Chinese outpost. She knew the military had always been the first outpost of colonialism, and culture and the arts shortlisted as the last, but she thought the Hong Kongers really did not know who they were. Unlike the Indians who had centuries of culture to fall back on when it regained its independence in 1947, Hong Kong was nothing but an offshore spit when the British acquired it in 1842, until the refugee influx from Mao's communism in 1949, at least those who'd decided to take their chances with the British in Hong Kong rather than Chiang Kai-shek in Taiwan. In the last half century Hong Kong had been well situated to be the recipients of orphaned property and flight capitalism, its work management earning the benefits of the convulsive ownership changes during the decolonization of much of East and South Asia. Now it's Hong Kong's turn, but since the people didn't even start thinking about who they were until 1982, Ge thought, it might well be the first time in human history that a community's going to completely colonize itself. Politically retarded, it's going to have to wear two faces all the time now, that of a master and that of a slave, and not know the difference.

For now though, Ge found a weekly calendar of duplicate bridge games in *The South China Morning Post,* and decided to take the ferry over to Central for the game that evening.

31. THE ROBO RIVER

Even from a distance, when his car crested the final hill onto a view of the top of the Grand Coulee Dam and the backed-up Columbia River renamed Franklin D. Roosevelt Lake, the scale was astonishing. Four little towns surrounded this dam in east central Washington, Grand Coulee, Coulee Dam, Elmer City and Electric City with a combined population less than a fourth of the Heart Mountain internment camp. G wanted to stay close to the dam, but not below it—so he found a room at the Four Winds in Grand Coulee just above the dam, a bed and breakfast converted from an engineers' dormitory during the dam's construction more than a half century ago.

He got out the maps, charts and books, and booted up a chat room window with Amy on his laptop for questions arising. There it was, the dam itself, a thick black bar across most maps originating in the United States, that iconic code that both transformed the cultural into the natural and constructed a historical narrative at the same time. Seemingly objective representations with no ideological underpinnings, they were suspiciously too good to be true. Amy agreed. Distances, elevations and bends in the river appeared objective and innocent enough; but when they were mixed with landing strips, surveyed range and township lines and especially road under construction symbols, an author with a specific agenda and a subjective narrative began to emerge. The Columbia River had been dammed here, a bold black stroke across the water's blue line adjacent to the Spokanes and the Confederated Colvilles. Marked *Coulee Dam National Recreation Area*, it sat alongside churches (with or without steeples), schoolhouses, post offices and Walmarts sharing the same significance, history and permanence.

Amy: you gotta be kiddin'
G: just look at the damned map
G: see if you can find if anything's gone wrong
Amy: like what
G: historically, engineering error, human error, unexpected shifts
Amy: back to you in an hour

G stepped out of the Four Winds for a break and took a walk down the street, just in time for the Laser Light Show authorized by Congress to enhance visitors' appreciation of this federal project. Beamed onto a cascading, bubbling-white water surface covering the dam face itself, it was an impressive and repetitious 40-minute display of moving light, its text filled with jumping dollar signs, jobs, cheap hydroelectric power, irrigation, flood control and recreation, hunting and fishing and jet skis, with Neil Diamond singing *We're coming to America, today*, filling in the silent spaces in the narrative. The vacationing crowd that nearly outnumbered the residents, they never stopped cheering from the beginning to the end.

G: you ready
Amy: got some stuff
G: shoot
Amy: idaho's teton dam built in 1975 under lies—4 to 10 benefit ratio—totally collapsed in less than year—engineering error—operating error
G: what else
Amy: 11 high dams on columbia—grand coulee, chief joseph,

wells, rocky reach, rock island, wanapum, priest rapids, mcnary, john day, dalles, bonneville—18,000mw total generating cap

G: what else

Amy: off columbia's main stem, more than 500—want the list

G: save for later

G: what else

Amy: mostly army corp, then usbr, a few puds—am sending email with attachment for grand coulee, and surprise, surprise, china's three gorges dam too

But Amy's chat door did not click shut; she's still on.

G: there's something else

Amy: surprise, surprise—near disaster march 14, 1952—1 upstream tube left open in error—flooding both powerhouses—half turbines running under water—supply to kaiser al rolling and reduction plants cut off—steam plants as far as puget sound took up slack for housewives' dinners

G: wow

Amy: wow is right

G: how long did it last

Amy: just one day

G: more tomorrow same time, bye

Amy: i'll try, bye

By the time G turned on his laptop before dawn the next morning, Amy's email with the attachment was waiting for him.

	Grand Coulee	*Three Gorges*
Structural height	167 m	185 m
Crest length	1,592 m	2,150 m
Generating capacity	6,494 mW	17,680 mW
Reservoir length	243 km	600 km
Reservoir capacity	11,795 m3x106	39,000 m3x106
Navigation	N/A	Twin 5-stage locks (20 m lift p/stage)
Construction period	9 years	18 years (est)

Concrete content   11,975,520 y3   22,910,000 m3

Putting it all together then, the Columbia River had eleven high dams that controlled its flow from its elevation of 1,290 feet at the Grand Coulee through its 596-mile journey to the Pacific Ocean. Hail the Robo River.

As a Democrat, Franklin Roosevelt had championed it as a purgation of national despair and unemployment, even as the president of the American Society of Civil Engineers saw it no more useful than Egypt's pyramids. Through a strategy of hoodwinking, both the US Corps of Engineers and Congress, FDR and the Bureau of Reclamation secured a blank check that paid for everything, from the tens of thousands of jobs in the dam's construction period, to the tens of thousands more who settled on its irrigated farming and orchard acres, to cheap hydroelectric power.

From the 1930s Go-Go years of the Grand Coulee to the John Day of 1968, thirty six dams went up on the Columbia and its tributaries, with nary a thought for their impact on the environment or people already living there. We're not talking about an Indian burial site here and there, but entire communities totally destroyed, such as the Wanapums and the Sanpoils, people who were not meant to survive, but did. This, then, was the second conquest and colonization of the West: the first was the cavalry, the second was the dam. What was once the spiritual lifeline had been changed into an economic workhorse with its implicit ideology. Some even argued that the Grand Coulee won WWII for the US by providing the high energy needed for the processing of aluminum needed for Boeing's B-17s and B-29s.

G: can you get comparative numbers on power rates
Amy: already have them, domestic rates in dollars in kwh—from the columbia, washington water power .03892, clearwater power .0618; on the east coast, con ed .031, western mass elec .029
G: don't believe it—double check
Amy: more than that, from multiple sources
Amy: note douglas, chelan and grant puds charge less—.02133

G: consortia on line buy and sell
Amy: whatever the market will bear

Here too, the lie was exposed. The power rates on the East Coast a good 2,000 miles away from these ideological dams were lower. Looking at the dam, now, out the window of a small diner in Grand Coulee, G thought the residents did not look particularly proud of this vanity project that had promised them a chance at a decent life. Instead, they looked as if they couldn't wait to get away, as most of their troubled and conflicted children already have, thrown in any direction to the exhausted conjuries of Spokane, Missoula, Boise or SLC. Rooted here where their options have been usurped and dreams wedged in the kink of a deep glacial slippage, they were walking around like aliens from another planet, or prisoners from this one on non-sustainable work release passes selling postcards, gifts, souvenirs and neon condoms at mini marts, boat docks and holding-tank dumps. In the restaurants and at the gas station G listened to their mimetic conversations with each other, their subjects always within the stray of the weather map and high school football prospects under the fall, Friday night lights. On another early evening walk from the Four Winds, G was astonished to see a man in the hillside to the west edge of town, hiding in the shallows of the mountain willows and talking to himself. Shading his eyes from the setting sun for a clearer view, G saw that this man with a checkered flannel shirt was actually whispering to a rusting tractor.

G imagined a Boeing B-52 *Stratofortress*, the four twin-engined weapon of indiscriminate mass destruction and slaughter, dropping its entire load of conventional explosives on this dam, but doubted it would have any significant impact. Desperate, he fantasized someone driving the *Sea Shepherd* up the entire length of the Columbia River, up the fish ladders of all of its eleven high dams, and then ramming the Grand Coulee from the upstream side. Shaking himself awake into this moment, he wondered if there was there anything, anything at all, that could be done to reverse this process that has turned the environment and the lives of people to shit.

32. 200 FERRARIS

Ge was astonished by the approaching, late capitalist skyscrapers on Central's waterfront as the green-and-white *Day Star* ferry took her across the harbor—the banks, hotels, restaurants and shopping malls that'll make any consumer happy. In contrast, she was reminded of a post-Tiananmen[2] required work unit political study session in which the topic was entitled *Scientific Socialism Reveals that the Main Historical Trend is that Socialism is Replacing Capitalism and that in the Last Twenty Years the Presence and Development of the Socialist System Has Made an Enormous Contribution toward the Progress of Both Humanity and World Peace.* Impossible! One Country, Two Systems seemed unimaginable to her when the culture in the Mainland and Hong Kong seemed totally incompatible. Unless of course, the leaders are so out of touch they don't know they are—and Deng Xiaoping's consumer terrorism has emerged the winner, prompting a material struggle between adults two or three generations apart. Unless of course China was not a country at all, but an adjective used to collate a series of geographical spaces, each with its own identifiable characters that resist and defy any use of a noun. She turned to look at the passengers around her, but could not understand who they were or what they represented, be they Asian, European,

American, Canadian or Australian.

Finding the bridge club between a former juvenile prison, a police precinct station and post office a short walk uphill from the ferry terminal was easy. But as soon as she took the elevator up and walked into the playing area, Ge was uncomfortably aware that everyone was staring at her, especially at her shoes. The only other woman in the room smiled and welcomed her, asking if she needed a partner. Ge said that she didn't play, but wanted to learn about the game.

"I'm Kavita," she said in English, "and that's Jackie, my partner, on the cell phone in the corner by the window. You're very welcome to sit behind me and kibitz. You're not from Hong Kong, are you?"

Ge wondered if her shoes had given her away, and explained that she was on vacation from Chengdu, being very careful about her English.

Kavita smiled. She had been to Chengdu last fall on vacation. "Maybe after the game we could go out for a drink and visit."

Within the first two sets, Ge had begun to understand the procedures of the game: the coded auction, the play of each deal, the scoring. Then this same deal was passed to the next table and played again by different players to yield a comparative score at the end of the session. It appeared some of the codes were artificial and complicated, and from their frowns and snorts, some players didn't appear to remember all of them.

It was the numbers component of the game that attracted Ge, particularly its distribution probabilities. Four suits, ranked clubs, diamonds, hearts, spades, and the conglomerate no trump. Each suit had thirteen cards. Each player had thirteen cards. Numbered one to thirteen, Ge spotted six primes, 1, 3, 5, 7, 11, 13. It appeared very important for the declarer and both of the defenders to know if not the exact distribution of each of these suits, then at least its approximation. But it also appeared to Ge that such information is based on a number no greater than 13, and that knowing how many spades there are in one hand will infinitely limit its distribution remaindered in the other three hands. But what are the total possible combinations, Ge started to compute in her head, starting with the first player. Without a calculator, she thought it would take her all night, but she approximated it to 635×10^9. Then the second player, to 8×10^9. Then the third, to 10×10^6. Finally the total, probably in the 52^{27} range. Would 13 into four hands be easier, she asked herself. By the fifth round, Ge had worked out only the significant patterns, 4-4-3-2, 4-3-3-3, 5-3-3-2, 5-4-3-1, 5-4-2-2, 6-3-2-2 and 6-4-2-1 accounting for more than 80% of the time, a simple probability exercise. Probably don't need to know more than that, Ge wrote in Chinese in the margin.

"What're you doing, Ge," Kavita asked.

"Oh, nothing, just putting together some numbers about this game."

"You seem quite engrossed. Are you sure you haven't played this game before?"

"Absolutely, totally."

Kavita and Jackie had come in second, behind the only other woman and her partner, in a field of seventeen tables of men, who were still trying to guess Ge's background and where she had found her shoes.

At the Foreign Correspondents' Club three blocks away where Kavita's a member, the two of them were drinking ginger ale for Kavita and green tea for Ge. Ge wanted to know if Kavita's considered a foreigner to be a member.

"No, but I string for several foreign newspapers and magazines. I'm third generation, Punjabi. My father came as a soldier and died in the defense of Hong Kong against the Japanese in 1941. And you?"

Ge explained that she had a degree in numbers, but since she did not want to teach, she'd been working on the dam project. "I work on the computer modeling of sedimentation problems with the dam design," she said.

"The Three Gorges Project?"

Ge nodded and took a sip of her green tea.

"Is anyone listening, I mean. I'm sorry Ge, it's part of my nature to pursue such issues."

"That's all right. My supervisor listens, and for the time being that's all we can hope for."

"What do you think about bridge now? You were taking quite

a few notes."

"It looks like a game I'd want to play. I was working out some distribution patterns."

"Oh," Kavita raised her eyebrows. "Can I see them?"

Kavita examined Ge's notepad flipped open to the page of significant patterns. "So these numbers represent more than 80%? Whatever happened to 4-4-4-1?"

"That's only about three percent of the time."

"I'd think it'll be more often, but then, you should know."

Ge wanted to know why the two of them were still attracting people's stares, even at the FCC, "where they know who you are."

"They're staring at you. But both of us at five foot nine or ten, that's very unusual for Chinese and Indian women, at least who they're used to. Plus we're not in the company of men, a metaphor they rely on in Hong Kong. And besides," she added, "these are journalists who are into looking at the unusual."

"But I mean, out there I'm stared at all the time, from the hotel lobby to the restaurant to the bookstore, to the ferry, everywhere in Hong Kong."

Yes, she was traveling alone. And her shoes, those light, black canvas slip intos can only mean she's from the country. But mostly because she didn't look like a Chinese Canadian, or a Chinese American, like she should because she's so tall, someone who had just spent a couple of weeks somewhere in China trying to find their roots, Kavita said. And failing to find any experience they can understand or identify, they flee to Hong Kong, the diaspora safe harbor, like Taipei or San Francisco, or Miami for the Cubans.

"Kavita, you are just like my friend Tang Li, such ruthless criticism of everything!"

"Maybe you're right. But look," she continued. They are torn between the Western media's presentation of China as a scourge to human rights and their own failure to find anything they can form an intellectual or emotional attachment to. To do so would require having to give up too much that's dear to middle class America, especially its perceived entitlement to ownership and continuity, property and permanence.

"Look Ge, they could not find any value in taking pictures of their parents' or grandparents' birthplace decades of political and cultural cycles later, and so they come to Hong Kong on their way home, the closest place they can get a hot shower anytime they want one."

The waiter came with a second pot of water.

"And you," Ge asked. "What about you?"

"What d'you mean what about me?" Hong Kong's the only place Kavita had ever known, except for her many trips every year. "But it's crazy here, probably more than most others, especially during this transition period."

There had been reports that the HK Polytechnic University was considering starting a department of Mao studies in anticipation of the 1997 handover, and that members of the 200 Ferraris club with less than fifty miles of highway to drive on were thinking about disbanding its chartered organization.

"We have that too. A newspaper reported a technical school teacher in Quizhou Province with a Mao tchotchkes collection of 19,000 varieties of 34,000 badges. But Kavita, what do they look like, these Chinese Canadians and Chinese Americans who could not find their roots?"

"They're usually under 30, disappointed and have run out of money. And they don't understand Hong Kong. But then, who does, including Hong Kongers. We didn't use to worry about it, but since 1982! Everyone's beginning to collect old photographs and trying to find some hints of their history in them."

Then they talked about the collectors of antiquity, there in Hong Kong as well as China. "If they want materiel antiquity," Kavita said firmly enough to turn a few heads at the usually sophisticated FCC crowd of seasoned journalists, "they can go to Taiwan and haul them back, or reclaim them from centuries of Christian missionaries, those pot hunters who took them home for souvenirs."

It was important for Ge to have made friends with Kavita, but it was also time for her to return to Chengdu. What she now understood was that Mao's revolution tried to give the Chinese some human dignity, but the result gave them the right to be irresponsible and had in fact legitimated the pissant moron. And of her work on the dam? Ge well knew the vast impossibility of it.

Ge knew enough to avoid the claptrap of piling all of life's dissonance and contradictions on the bane of capitalism or skein of communism. There will be change in China, she told herself, slow and piecemeal, mostly banal and unnoticed, but things will change. Right now though, it's better to go back and muddle and negotiate her way through it, rather than run away from her endowment and seek asylum in the nearest American consulate, like the astrophysicist Fang Lizhi. Ah, the determination of vanity wrapped in illusory envelopes.

33. C-4

If the cavalry made the first conquest and colonization of the West, and the dam its re-conquest and re-colonization, then Brigham Young's efforts in Utah pre-dated both. When he came down from the hilltop in 1846 and announced *This is it*, this was the place, this was where the church will set its new foundations along City Creek, few people today remember that his next breath muttered *Get out the shovels*. It is no wonder then, that today both the US Corps of Engineers and the Bureau of Reclamation have an abundance of Latter-Day Saints members. It took old Brigham only a moment to realize the importance of water in the West, that smart cookie.

G had learned in the last couple of weeks that in order to understand the West, one had to understand water, its presence and, more significantly, its absence. The more than 500 dams in the Pacific Northwest did not reflect our understanding of it. Conserve, conserve. Every American was a conservationist. To conserve was to save it, to husband it, so G thought. But somehow here in the West where the presiding ideology hinged on the assumption that not to use it was to waste it—to conserve meant to make use of it. Use every bit of it; let nothing go to waste. Use that water. Find every waterway big enough to warrant a continuous blue line on maps and stamp as many black bars across it as possible.

Here on the massive Columbia, the eleven American dams and three Canadian dams (Mica, Revelstoke, Keenleyside) on its main stem and the more than 500 on its tributaries not only held the water hostage by the turn of a valve, but committed most of its residents into believing that the collateral damage to both the environment and to humans was somehow sustainable and worth the price.

For two days now G had wanted to know if the entire process could be reversed. He started looking for a River Dragon to appear and remove all these dams, at least the eleven high ones on the Columbia. First he thought about the effects of a Boeing B-52 dropping its entire 60,000-pound load of conventional ordnance, but doubted its effectiveness on 11,975,521 cubic yards of reinforced concrete, enough concrete to build a sidewalk four feet wide and four inches thick to go around the world twice at the equator.

What about a set of torpedoes targeting the upriver side of the dam face at forty feet below the water level. Impractical, and like the B-52 load, it wouldn't be enough. Imagine getting his hands on some outdated military surplus, or if lucky and with a lot of money and slick networking, something big from China's rogue arms manufacturer Norinco and going out on Lake Roosevelt on a moonless night in a raft and launching them without the appropriate aiming devices and blowing up the Spring Canyon boat launch, its concession stands and Porta-Potties. It'll be a form of symbolic guerrilla or fifth column action. G wanted to do something more than that; he wanted to do something that could not be reversed.

G could wait for nature to take its course, like the Teton Dam in Idaho that collapsed in 1976 and wiped out Sugar City and Rexburg immediately below it. But that would be unlikely to happen, he concluded while staring at the dam's massive concrete structure from the visitors' center below the dam.

The night before, Amy had emailed G a list outlining the Grand Coulee's WWII security measures designed to interdict fifth columnist attempts of terrorism: severely restricting visitor access; quadrupling federal guards to 65, including deputizing five of them as US Marshals; erecting a 10-foot metal fence around both main access roads as well as the two switchyards; placing a heavy log boom across the reservoir a quarter mile above the dam; assigning the US Coast Guard and four speed boats for additional waterway security; constructing fifteen guard stations at strategic locations; installing floodlights; partial flooding of the pumping plant behind the discharge tunnels and pump inlet pipes; building concrete bulkheads inside the dam to limit internal flooding; equipping all doors with industrial locks; adding an alarm system augmented with an air raid siren system that could have been heard up to two miles away; using a new ID system that included photo and payroll number.

G examined these security measures one more time and concluded that he had been entirely wrong in his basic approach. He had noticed this time that this dam had been designed to withstand sabotage from the outside. Just maybe it'll be a lot easier from the inside. Maybe he could beat Interior Secretary Bruce Babbitt to it, who had just said at a Montana Trout Unlimited fundraiser dinner last week, "I would love to be the first Secretary of the Interior to tear down a really large dam."

It'll have to be done with explosives on the inside, placed maybe 200 feet below the water level, in one of the offices or storerooms or lunchrooms or toilets at a level between the turbines and Westinghouse generators. (Oh yeah, G's known about the six 67,500 hp Westinghouse generators for some time, but realizing his connection to it, however indirect, he and the author have kept this information from you until now.) Some concentrated explosive a person can roll into a sightseer's fanny pack, something just big enough to initiate a *piping*, a few drops squeezing through a pinhole, before the pressure behind expands the hole into a growing pipe until the weight and force of the water explodes the dam. It could take hours, or even a few days.

Ah, C-4. G was already familiar with the principles of making this incredibly strong and illegal explosive in any ordinary kitchen, although he'll need some additional specific information for time, weight, volume and temperature. He'll need to get his hands on three easily available chemicals. The first'll be inexpensive $NaAl(SO_4)_2$ from a grocery store. (You don't think G's going to give you the real ingredients, do you?) Next'll be the sometimes difficult to obtain $KHC_4H_4O_6$, a syrupy, white liquid, unless one has access to a well-stocked gourmet kitchen store. The third is the common $C_{40}H_{75}NO_9$ that can be picked up in any hardware or paint store in the country.

G also knew that to combine these materials, the $NaAl(SO_4)_2$ must go through a drying process that must not exceed $150°$ F, turning it into prill. This drying process is continued with saturating the prill with $C_{40}H_{75}NO_9$ for about three minutes until the brown sludge is removed. The liquid is then drained, and the excess eliminated with gentle stirring and heating, again for about three minutes. Then the prill must be ground to a powder consistency, possibly with a coffee grinder, and sealed in an airtight container.

The final mixing process requires one-third $KHC_4H_4O_6$ by volume, or two parts $KHC_4H_4O_6$, to five parts $NaAl(SO_4)_2$ by weight. Augmented by a #6 or #8 detonation cap, and it's ready to go, with a shelf life of about a month, just about long enough for G to find a way down into some lunchroom 200 feet below the waterline at a level between the turbines and the generators.

And what if it worked? A piping eventually leading to a complete blowout? What'll happen to the 11,795,000,000 cubic meters of water held back behind the dam at Roosevelt Lake? Will it instantly form a towering mass of water half a mile wide, half a mile high and twenty-one miles thick? From the Grand Coulee Dam the Columbia River meanders some fifty miles easterly to the next dam, the Chief Joseph, before it makes a slow, thirty-mile U-turn south before the next, the Wells Dam. Will the fight-no-more-forever Chief Joseph let this water through? Will this wall of water with a velocity of more than sixty miles an hour manage the U-turn? Will 3,060,408,754,160,000 gallons of water be enough to flush out all the black bars across the Columbia River—the Grand Coulee, Chief Joseph, Wells, Rocky Reach, Rock Island, Wanapum, Priest Rapids, McNary, John Day, The Dalles and Bonneville—until they reach the Pacific Ocean near Astoria? Will this water gather enough volume and velocity to duplicate the collapse of Lake Missoula some sixteen thousand years ago, its magnitude stripping everything down to bedrock, channeling new scablands and carving out new coulees and potholes? There is only one way to find out, G thought, as he paid cash for a 10-pound bag of $C_{40}H_{75}NO_9$ at Spokane's North Division K-Mart.

Daughter of Ice, Echo of Wind, Orphan of Fire, the Columbia, steadfast in still and roiling waters.

Part Three

No man lives simply his own life. He lives in great
part the lives of his ancestors, of his parents.
He lives the lives of his children and the lives of those
who are to follow them.
(Ralph Ellison, "Commencement Address")

34. CONTINUOUS HARMONIC FUNCTIONS

It's a nightmare I've seen a number of times before, while doing anything—brushing my teeth, picking up an eggplant at the market, or determining a holomorphic function within the boundary conditions $u^+ = f^+(t) + C_K$, $u^- = f^-(t) + C_K$ on L_K, $k = 1,2...,p,$. Each time I would jump back for a better look, each time verifying that there was no other way of seeing it than through this fiction. It's always the same each time, carefully tucked between sleep and insomnia, this dream in which I'm sleeping fully clothed, ready to wake up at the slightest change in temperature, just in case. I've even tried to avoid it by sleeping naked, on my other side, with my hands between my legs, or challenging that mythical thermometer that makes believe all our bodies are alike at 98.6°. I can't remember if any of that did any good, because when the nightmare occurred, as it did last night, there's no remembering anything else and no stopping it. And nothing can be done to change its course, its eleven, or is it thirty-nine billion, cubic meters of water roaring down the basalt canyon at over 260,000 cubic meters per second. I woke up completely wrecked, my body too exhausted for sleep, the dam quite dead, my toes still nudging the few foamy puddles of muddy water left on the new shore. This was how I came to work this morning, my body heavy and unbalanced, ignoring Chengdu's increasingly maddening morning traffic, the guards' security check and supervisor Zhang's nod.

For weeks now, that civil engineer Plutonium Chang had been pushing, pushing for his flood-control project, as if the primary purpose of the dam had been dedicated to promoting his personal career. He had consistently dismissed the lower-ranking environmental department's persistent warning that soil erosion is serious in most of the counties in the Yangtze's basin, in both Hubei and Sichuan provinces, and that this continuing self-perpetuating degradation would create siltation problems for the dam's reservoir's storage capacity. He had also ignored the anticipated social consequences that relocating more than two million people away from the dam's new water level will rent the family fabric and create yet another permanent underclass in the urban centers of Chengdu, Chongqing, Wuhan, Nanjing and Shanghai.

"We have to hold the water back in the peak months, June, July, August." Then this craven apparatchik added, as if we were children, "Do you know how many people are drowned annually by the Changjiang's floods?"

We kept on pointing out that during such peak flows it was imperative to keep the reservoir level low so that the sediment would be discharged. Zhang even introduced a mathematical model developed by the Academy of Hydraulics, using an equation that I had not been very comfortable with, $J = 0.0062D_{50}^{1.4}/(Q/B)^{0.92}$, to show that when the Changjiang has reached its sedimentation equilibrium state, the gradient will be about 0.00007, which is only 35% of the original. Chang would not even look at the chalkboard; he sipped his tea and looked out the window instead.

Then he turned, looking straight at me, and added his ultimate insult, "You're not even working with real numbers."

After several angry moments of heavy breathing and no one looking at anyone else, Zhang asked, "If we impounded the water during peak flows, both the clear and the turbid, won't we be merely transferring the flood potential from the lower Changjiang to the upper Changjiang?"

"We have to work with him." It's Zhang's voice behind me.

Realizing that I had been sitting in front of my console for untold minutes staring at the screen saver and doing absolutely nothing, I turn to face him in the frozen persimmon flush of embarrassment.

"We must work with him, or else quit completely," he corrects himself.

"Yes, I agree," I manage to say. "But it's the tedium and waste of it all."

Zhang laughs, but I know he is in agreement.

But how can we effectively stand together behind sound principles against someone's monster project? It seems what we do here is totally irrelevant. Why are we doing any work at all, when Li Peng and Jiang Zemin at an official ceremony had already cut off the Yangtze at 3:13pm for the coffer dam last November 8? Whether it's Plutonium Chang's recommendations that's going to be accepted or ours, it's going to be compromised again at the next level, and again at the level after that with the politicians and the banks.

Everyone in the world wants cheap hydroelectric power, but don't they know they can have it without building the biggest vanity dam in the world? A dam like that'll never be allowed to go up in the US today, not like in the Go-Go Years of the 1930s, the Canadian Earthscan email message said this morning. It also mentioned the Americans are going through the slow and painful process of drawing down and breaching their high dams — starting with four on the Snake River, in fifty years there'll be nothing left but concrete husks littering the major waterways of the American West. Instead, such corporate greed is being played out in the developing waters of South America and here in Asia, with the full consent of the indigenous fascist party in power.

There's nothing we can do besides voice our opposition to whoever cares or cares not to listen, sometimes at great risk to our careers for sure, and sometimes to our personal safety as well. For supervisor Zhang, loss of pension, death? For me, loss of my Qinghua diploma, imprisonment? We can also stall in our computations, sabotage tests, as we've been doing more and more when the moron civil engineer Plutonium Chang isn't watching.

We all know the completion of this dam is inevitable, that this is another horrendous instance in our history in which we will suffer for generations — deprived of life on the river, life in the river and life from the river, and the river itself that connects us to the other life forms in the world, this excruciating loss of dreams, wishes, and yes, lies too. Unless some radical activist emerges and does something about it. But instead of chaining himself to a sluice gate under construction now, he will patiently wait fifteen years until the dam's completion in 2016 to blow up the whole thing and himself with it with two kilos of fresh plastic explosives that he's rolled into his sightseer's fanny pack, in the Chinese way. I grow more pessimistic by the day, and I am tired. Every piece of porcelain in my kitchen is either chipped, cracked, broken or mended.

"Ge, you don't look so good. Why don't you go up to the Dujiangyan and talk to our friend Weng before he retires," Zhang interrupts my meandering. "Get another perspective on this."

Zhang has been thinking about his own retirement that he's put off for years, I can see it in his eyes. For the last few months he's even stopped wearing his tie. But he keeps on coming in every day, as if his presence alone is enough to keep people like Plutonium Chang from getting their way immediately. And it has, this willful act of resistance. Maybe that is all we can ever do.

And yes, it will be a chance to see the Min River again in this magical month of October, and to talk to the patient Weng, high up there in the hills where the changing leaves are singing, giving us a space between sentences. And yes, I am thankful that Zhang has been compassionate without resorting to metaphors that can only serve to deflect our attention from the issue.

35. CNN

From the bicycle stalls inside the front gate, I can see a gathering in front of the television monitor through the opened windows of the dining hall and feel the electricity of the collective silence and its intermittent eruption of wonder. By the time I step inside the building, it looks as if everyone in our division is gathered here, even the two guards who have abandoned their security posts at the front and rear gates. Zhang and Chang are the closest to the monitor, and everyone is watching a satellite-beamed CNN Special Report.

The monitor shows a map, tight shot of the northern section of the state of Washington, with Spokane to the east. The Columbia River's bold blue line zigzags from north to south, and six short, black bars cross it, marking the six major dams before the river runs to the edge of the map just north of Yakima. As Bernard Shaw reads the story, the top two black bars blink and then disappear.

"... local law enforcement agencies suspect that the Grand Coulee was destroyed by a well-organized terrorist group possibly linked to various radical or anarchist environmental or green organizations ..."

Plutonium Chang starts to translate the narrative, but Zhang shuts him up in the clear, perfect future tense of Chinese. "We all know English in here, Chang."

The two black bars reappear, blinking, and the top one is replaced by a blinking, small red bubble.

"... but at this point no one has taken credit for what the President has called a cowardly act that has taken a number of lives downriver ..."

Zhang walks towards me, pale and visibly shaken.

"... the Federal Bureau of Investigation has been joined by units from the US Marshals and the Bureau of Alcohol, Tobacco and Firearms, as well as the Washington National Guard providing transportation for an orderly evacuation, medical care and temporary housing ..."

"Maybe we should go outside, into the fresh air," Zhang says, taking me by the elbow.

"... a spokesman for the Army Corps of Engineers in Walla Walla has estimated that more than a trillion cubic yards of water from Lake Roosevelt was released by the collapse of the Grand Coulee, and the force of the rampaging water tore down the next dam along the river, the Chief Joseph. A wide bend in the river spilled most of the water westward into the plains, and the next dam, the Wells, held fast.

"The final death toll will not be available for weeks or months. The spokesman indicated that due to the effective alarm system and early detection of the dam's initial slow leak, that number is expected to be miraculously lower than the one hundred and thirty six drowned in one afternoon of flash flooding on the Colorado's Big Thompson River in 1976.

"It has been reported that an elderly couple refused to be evacuated. They had decided to stay in their home, reminiscent of Harry Truman during the Mt. St. Helens volcanic eruption in the same state in 1980."

Among murmurs and heads nodding and shaking, Zhang steadies me by the elbow and walks me out of the crowded dining hall into the sunshine.

"What the Americans won't do to correct their mistakes," he stammers along the way. "Build it up, knock it down, like children in a nursery or on the beach. You live by it; you die by it."

My breathing returns in the harsh sunlight of the courtyard. I hear the Columbia River's echo forming a question for me here on the Yangtze, and for my parents on the Yellow River a few years ago—how we live in it, dispersed as we are flesh in all of its eddies. We live like this over the river's edge, this wider water glittering with teeming assertion, our reason collecting at the constantly changing waterline, where only a vague shadow marks the difference between abundance and exploitation.

36. RIFTS

The computer's taking its time booting up this morning, and I'm holding my breath for what seems like hours thumbing through a road atlas so old the Interstate system doesn't exist. Come on, come on, one eye on the monitor that's starting to frizzle and glow and the other on panhandle Idaho, the St. Joe National Forest, up the St. Joe River and its cutthroat trout, Red Ives, Simmons Peak, over the hump and down into St. Regis, Montana. Pop, pop, frizzle, and a prompt backtracked to <wxyz@ public2.east.cn.net> with the message *Please mark on your calendars retirement dinner for Zhang and Weng*. Huh? I don't know anyone with this *public2.east* address in China, and I sure don't know anyone by *Zhang* or *Weng*, retirement or not. And *wxyz*, sure, why not, the Chinese have appropriated the tail end of the Roman alphabet anyway, why not: *Wan, Weng, Wang, Wei, Wei, Wu, Xia, Xiao, Xie, Xu, Xue, Xin, Yang, Ye, Yi, Yuan, Yan, Yao, Zhang, Zhao, Zhou, Zou, Zhu, Zheng.* Anyone for triple-word, triple-letter Scrabble?

These little disturbances have been occurring with greater frequency lately, a prevailing fiction that seems to be taking over my life. Even my committed cousin Ted, for instance, has quit his journalism career, convinced that whatever truth that's out there today is totally subverted by editors and publishers in the grand tradition of the Henry Luce publications. He's taped to the top of his computer monitor a statement another Ted, Teddy White, had written about his coverage of the war in China during WWII—*Any resemblance to what is written here and what is printed in* Time Magazine *is purely coincidental*. And he's moved to writing what he calls semi-documentary pieces that would narrow the ambiguous gulf between the subject and the writer, somewhere just short of fiction. Amy thinks it's just a matter of hours before he'll turn to writing novels.

Since Westinghouse has been sold and reconfigured twice in the last decade, my work has become increasingly managerial. The contractual work has moved into the areas of telecommunications systems, public health and environmental engineering, especially the containment, transportation and eventual disposal of lethal toxic wastes produced by the Department of Defense at well over a ton a minute, more than that of DuPont, Exxon and Union Carbide combined. Rumor has it that sections of the Army's chemical R&D department at its Aberdeen Proving Ground float on so much picric acid that it has requisitioned a flotilla of pontoons from the Navy just for getting around the installation.

But look here, I'm no fool: I'm well aware that at any given moment our work can be instantly compromised and reversed from its intended civilian purpose and put to a military application. Right now I'm involved in the computing modeling designed to predict and track the migration of various leaking toxic contaminants. Who's running this show, civilian or the military? And when something major goes wrong in its application, where will be responsibility placed and who will be prosecuted? Certainly not the Pentagon. And since the government's interest presumably is in justice and the pursuit of this goal, sorry buddy, you're out on your own, buddy.

The emailed retirement dinner reminder doesn't include a RSVP, but maybe I should write back just to see where it'll take me. Type R, then Got it. Time and place? Signed G with the automatic return route of <G.G@PSS.Westinghouse.com>. Control X and then Y to send it.

It comes back *Undeliverable*—this is going to be an incomplete story, unlike others in here, some important enough to be repeated to circumvent the amnesia of the careless or lazy reader, those with a few missing ticks, or the privileged buffered with so much superfluous abundance that they don't have to pay any attention at all. I scroll the screen back to the initial message and sure enough, it is addressed to me, but the listserv has not been included. My eyes wander to a black ink spot on the sleeve of my shirt, and imagine a stranger with the same sleeve, the sleeve a stranger passing behind me so close he's almost brushing against me. He stops and whispers *Are you nuts?* His words touch me so much to the point I want to follow him, matching his every step, embracing his version of things, the spaces of the possible, of renewal, of mutation, of movement, of regeneration — the spaces of reconciliation and birth.

The truth lies in tiny disembodied bits of such fluff hanging across someone's laundry line or around the tablecloth in a dirty restaurant or under the chair in someone's living room, in crinkled brows or understanding nods, in quiet talk or a small paragraph or an act of sudden violence, however small. It exists outside of you, but you have to see it and touch it and smell it and taste it, and even then you have to put it all together to recognize it, and even then it may not be what your neighbor sees, as such perceptions endanger their very survival.

At least the *Undeliverables* are flagged and returned to the sender who will then know that the story has been halted, sometimes only temporarily. Let me try another approach, forwarding the undeliverable. Type *F*, repeat the *wxyz* address, then Control *X* and *Y* and wait for verification. Yes, there it is, moved to *Sent Mail.*

37. PRISONER'S DILEMMA

> *The past is never dead. It's not even past.*
> (William Faulkner)

Congress has just passed a law making it a federal crime to publish any instructional material for the production of bombs or explosives of any kind. It is monitored and enforced by agents from both the Bureau of Alcohol, Tobacco and Firearms, as well as the Federal Bureau of Investigation. Since the detailed instructions for how I'd put together the pound of C-4 for blowing up the Grand Coulee had been included in the original narrative at my insistence, it poses a dilemma for the author, his agent, editor and publisher, and it may well involve copy editor, proofreaders, cover designer, printer, publicists, distributors and ultimately booksellers—a long queue of literary producers from author to seller manacled and summoned to appear before a US district court grand jury on a federal charge of conspiracy to cause harm to both body and mind.

Are the potential rewards worth the risks? Is there a mathematical solution to this conflict without engaging in prodigious arithmetical calculations that would make us go mad? Is there anyone at Santa Monica's RAND Corporation who can provide a rational answer to these questions? Take the principals, the author and the publisher: a) if the author didn't include these instructions in the first place, there will be no crime, everyone will be happy, except me, this is my story; b) if the publisher chooses to censor pages 150 and 151, both the author and I will be unhappy; c) if the publisher does not vet these pages, just maybe both the ATF and the FBI will miss it or look the other way because this is fiction after all, and everyone will be happy. Except, except of course for Senator Jesse Helms who'll read this novel as the relentless political critique of American culture, and Senator Slade Gorton, the Grand Coulee Dam's in his state, for crissakes. So don't count on c) as a conciliatory outcome, folks. Step right up, turn to Matthew's Do to others what you would have them do to you, or Immanuel Kant's categorical imperative in which everyone believes in the same ethical behavior. Fat chance. We have a standoff here, the literal versus the metaphorical.

So where do we turn?
To the author? Fat chance.
That carnie is feigning a loss
of interest in this story.
Even when G has already
blown away the Grand Coulee
the author is thinking about
the essential difference

We kept on pointing out that
during such peak flows it was
imperative to keep the
reservoir level low so that
the sediment would be discharged
Zhang even introduced
a mathematical model developed
by the Academy of Hydraulics,

between the poet and the novelist, that essential difference. He's thinking that while the poet's interest does not go beyond just the idea of blowing up the dam, the novelist has to know exactly how to blow up the dam, and then contend with the consequence of eleven billion cubic meters of water charging down the Columbia towards the Pacific at 260,000 cubic meters per second, if it'll make the thirty-mile U-turn between Chief Joseph and Wells that is, if one two-pound brick of freshly made C-4 will take out all eleven dams on the Columbia River. The poet wants to party; but the novelist's the one who calls the friends together, picks up the refreshments and plugs in the music.

But before following the author to this party that may or may not take place — you know how unreliable these writers are about such things, poet or novelist — I must go back to what I've been exploring for the last two weeks, an article establishing some heritability estimators in the complete absence of genetic factors, if it can be done. Maybe it can be done, although the mathematical part will surely be criticized as merely convenient and not realistic. Scroll, scroll, to, here. $E(X_1 - X_2)^2 = E[(X_1 - u) - (X_2 - u)]^2 = V(X_1) + V(X_2) - 2Cov(X_1, X_2) = 2[V(X_1) - Cov(X_1, X_2)]$.

"We have to work with him." It's the division chief's voice behind me, and he's referring to our DOE liaison, our contract man.

It feels like the second time today that we've had this conversation. He's looking at me as if my body's been wrecked by nightmares and needs a break. He's also been questioning the work we've been instructed to do on determining the aerial spread of UX, the most deadly of all known lethal nerve agents. Ever since its deliberate release in a Tokyo subway tunnel about a decade ago, we've been pushed to calculate the morphology of its spread and methods for its containment.

"We must work with him, to make sure our findings can't be compromised for aggressive ends." He looks at me again and adds, "Hey G, you don't look so good. Why don't you take a few days off?"

Sure, why not, an opportunity for improvisation, a journey to somewhere, a place where we won't have to be so vigilant and things aren't coded, where there is life after all.

38. RIVERS

I've always wondered who were brave and stupid enough to write their thoughts on Beijing's Tiananmen[2] walls west of the Forbidden City in the short-lived Democracy Movement in November of 1978. What did they think they were doing, standing there singing with eyes closed, waiting for the democracy coin to tinkle into the can at their feet?

But then, what does a series of little dislocations matter after the original horror? Yes, yes, if you must know, in 1958 I was thirteen and old enough to know. My family was separated by the Great Leap Forward social programs of mobilizing the nation's will and energy. Later I found out that my parents had been sent to an agricultural commune along the Yellow River in Henan Province, one of the newly aggregated 26,000 rural communities designed to increase national productivity.

one more, this one a secret. In the top drawer of my dresser I keep a small lock box containing a current American Express card and a valid passport. I call this box *Gold Mountain*, in which I keep my mother's letters that were given

I was sent to a work camp of teenagers on higher ground in Shandong Province where we worked and slept with our hoe or pick. Sometimes in the evenings we talked philosophy when we weren't too tired, or in the tool shed when it was raining so hard we couldn't work in the fields. But I preferred to work alone, away from the children my age, especially when it was planting trees on the levee. I knew what I had to do, and I liked the work. A lunch box and seedlings in a dampened bag tied to my waist, a pick in my hand, I enjoyed it, except when the ground was hard away from the levee.

Some of the villagers had no concept of time or geography, and most of them were kind to us even though we didn't use the same language and needed an interpreter whenever a new policy was handed down from the county prefect, and that was every week.

emotional and intellectual reserves to be able to imagine the life lived by the banished, exiled and displaced. I'm not sure if I belong in that category, but I suspect that Amy would.

Over the centuries they had learned to please visitors, soldiers and officials and said what they wanted to hear, if only to avoid tax penalties. They measured time by the sun, and distance by the time it took to reach a designated horizon. They did not know anything about their neighbors of five or more centuries living only a few kilometers away, and definitely did not perceive of themselves as Chinese or any other macro grouping. Often they did not know their own given names or the names of others, except by nicknames and other invented names. So for two years I labored at this camp where the politics of the nation became the politics of the individual. *Changing the whole nation and changing one's life together* became the song.

One day an old woman I recognized came up to me when I was finishing up tamping down the soil on some seedlings and asked in perfect Mandarin, "Do you allow for improvisation in your life?"

I was speechless.

"I have been watching you, and you must go to a school. There is much you can do."

At that moment on the muddy levee, both the horizon and time became one in the late spring sunlight in maybe the only home I had known, before I was sent to school in Beijing.

In that imperfect reality, I learned that my parents had decided to stay in the village on the Yellow River when the flood warning scattered all the villagers to higher ground. They had chosen not to be relocated one more time, only to return in a month or two to the same life without hope. A neighbor's letter said that they had decided to stay, so that someone can explain what happened. They had decided to put their lives in the hands of the river and let the story take its own course.

The numbers show that millions died during this period from hunger, dislocation and despair. Who should we hold responsible—the architects of the program, or everyone who didn't say *No*? It seems all of our tragedies are authored, directed, performed and consumed by ourselves, so maybe there's no need to blame anyone else. And what are the personal consequences when the parents are dead and their children find out why years later? What happens to the children, imagining themselves onto the horror of a new page already less eternal?

39. SILHOUETTES

*We are haunted by our past, which clings
to us like strange, mystical lint. Of the past,
the mystery of family is the most beautiful,
the saddest, and the most inescapable of all.*
(W.P. Kinsella, *The Iowa Baseball Confederacy*)

Amy once said that most middle-classed Americans need extraordinary emotional and intellectual reserves to be able to imagine the life lived by the banished, exiled and displaced. I'm not sure if I belong in that category, but I suspect that Amy would point to my materiel accouterments—MIT degree, job with Westinghouse, car, apartment, insurance, who I hang out with, what I read—and conclude that it'll be difficult to deny it. But I suspect that spending one's summer vacation blowing up the fucking Grand Coulee Dam doesn't exactly fit this MO.

And you, reader, what about you? All right, all right, I'll give you one more piece so that there'll be nothing withheld. For once, Amy is wrong, too literal, where she pointed out on page 33 that I had made up the entire story about working for the St. Joe National Forest, all "maps and books," I believe she said. Uninterpreted raw data is meaningless, not fictions we can believe.

The truth is, I didn't make it up, the summers of 1963 and 1964, working fires mostly in Region 1 with the blister rust hotshot crew. Look it up. And that was before the two summers when I worked as a smokejumper out of Missoula's Jump Center. It was also a period when the CIA was at the base every weekend trying to snarl recruits for its covert work in Vietnam and Laos. I was never approached as a potential asset by these suits, and someone explained that it was because they thought slopeheads were all alike and couldn't be trusted. Sure that's true. You can look that up too. And tell Amy.

But you want more, the maggot that you are.

Okay, just one more, this one a secret. In the top drawer of my dresser I keep a small lock box containing a current American Express card and a valid passport. I call this box *Gold Mountain*, in which I also keep my mother's letters that were given to me by my mother's friend when she thought I was old enough to understand them. And I remember my mother, past the musty smell of these letters into the musty smell of a convalescent room when I was five, as she looked at me, sitting there upright in bed, the night she nearly wasn't there. I keep the credit card and passport handy in case I suddenly want to take off in a crass mythology and go visit her hometown, Liuhe in Jiangsu Province. But I know I won't—I just want to know that they're there so I can dream, uncompromising and clear. Once in a while I get out one of those letters and read it very carefully:

October 30

Dear Aunty—
 We arrived at Victoria three days ago. I was very tired after the long ride on the train. Now everything is set for sailing on November 4th. Because of the war, the sailing date has been delayed. Victoria is such a nice place that it is not so bad to spend a few days wondering here and there.
 The trip from Boston was more pleasant than I expected. Gregor behaved extremely well, having sound sleep every night, making friends with everyone on the train. From Montréal to Vancouver we met a whole car of English people who came from

England on their way to China and India. They are going to take the S.S. Empress of Canada too. So we have had and are going to have quite a group of companions. The men always talk politics in the smoking room and we, the ladies, have afternoon tea together everyday. In the sleeping car there is a small kitchen with gas and an icebox for passengers. This made it very convenient for me to prepare food for Gregor.

The Canadian Pacific Service is wonderful. They sent men to see us off at Boston and to meet us at Montréal, Vancouver and Victoria, taking care of our baggage and everything so it made it very easy not to have to bother about anything.

Chinese friends here have fixed a small but nice apartment for us. It is very nice as well as convenient, we enjoy the scenic view in the neighborhood and visit the beautiful gardens. I wish that we could stay here longer.

The snow-covered Canadian Rockies are grand. I have Never seen such a beautiful view before. If we can send the baby away, we like to spend a few days on the mountains.

We are waiting for sailing and shall write you on the boat.
With much love from all of us.

Kitty

40. *ARIETTA: ADAGIO MOLTO,*
SEMPLICE E CANTABILE

Both G and Ge have Type A blood, a rarity for Asians that would prevent them from giving blood for a majority of their gene pool. This doppelganger then has its limits. They follow each other, and I for one assume something can be communicated by the act of committing their stories to the page, word by word. Along with others who have tried it, Jean Paul, Aleksander Pushkin, Fedor Dostoevski, Joseph Conrad, Philip Roth and now Edmund Morris, we have merely imitated the original, Jesus of Nazareth, although some conventional theologian might well challenge the dual physical being. How else can we name it—biogenetic rift, parallel existence, the double, harmonic twins, parallax habitation, trans-habitation, crossed matrix, and jumbled coordinates?

On the lower tier, the variation would include Mary Shelley and R.L. Stevenson, as well as all spies, turncoats and bigamists. But that's another matter I'd prefer to leave be.

In looking over their shoulders at their monitors, I see that both G and Ge are submitting papers for the next International Conference on Fibonacci Numbers and Their Applications to be held year after next at Prague. It seems their papers have identical titles, *On the Minimal Center Covering Stars with Respect to GCD in Pascal's Pyramid and its Generalizations*, and proceed with the same notations and terminology. *Take any entry $X = n!/k_1!k_2!...k_m!$, where $n = k_1 + k_2 + ... + k_m$, inside Pascal's and relatively to X, we conveniently use the m–dimensional vector notation $(c_1, c_2, ...c_m) = (n + c_1 + c_2 + ... + c_m)!/(k_1 + c_1)!(k_2 + c_2)!...(k_m + c_m)!$ to represent any entry in the pyramid.*

Until then, then, I can only wish them the best of journeys. Travel on whispers of wind, and trust the silences and darkness that the rain leaves between two waters where we truly belong, one inside the other.

41. PRAGUE

They're here from all over the world: Turkey, China, Italia, Brunei, Germany, Grand-Duchy of Luxembourg, Poland, India, Japan, Yugoslavia, Scotland, Cyprus and the United States. Some sixty papers will be presented during this weeklong international conference in Prague, and G and Ge's papers On the Minimal Center Covering Stars with Respect to GCD in Pascal's Pyramid and its Generalizations are highlighted at the top of the program just below the keynote address.

To encourage audience discussion, the organizers of the conference have kept the individual presentations small. G and Ge have been assigned to different but adjoining rooms separated by a retractable, sliding door. There will be no yawns here, even though some of the theorems will rub elbows with each other in variously combined accents. This is not just a story—our perimeter of safety has disappeared, and things are waiting to be renamed. G and Ge's world, and indeed our world, has doubled. The only thing left is the proof, that illusive weapon.

Unknown to G, Ge gets up first and begins reading from her paper: *Take any entry X inside Pascal's triangle. Divide the six entries surrounding X into two sets S_1 and S_2 by taking these six entries alternately. Then the product of three elements in S_1 is equal to one in S_2.*

A few minutes later in the adjacent room, G continues the introduction: *This property was found by Hoggatt and Hansell, and called the hexagon property w.r.t. the product. The hexagon property w.r.t. GCD was also established by Hillman and Hoggatt, while this property does not hold w.r.t. LCM.*

Reading slower in her second language, Ge gets to the notations just as the dividing door starts retracting the separation between them. *Take any entry $X = n!/k_1!k_{-2}!...k_m!$* But in his native language, G catches up and finishes the sentence. *Where $n = k_1 + k_2 + ...+ k_m$, inside Pascal's pyramid consists of m-nomial coefficients.*

The dividing door has completely retracted, and both G and Ge stop reading and look up from their papers. Some in the audience are standing up, looking into the adjacent room and back. They look at G and Ge, and then at each other. They repeat this several times. They are more naive and simple-hearted than we had supposed mathematicians to be.

G and Ge are looking hard at each other, their breathing almost stopped. They are looking into the future, and into the past. And at this moment of moments they take a breath and look at each other, the audience, the author and the reader.

Photo by Ray Deng

Born in Boston, Alex Kuo spent most of World War II in China, followed by eight years in Hong Kong before returning to the United States. He has lived and worked most of his adult life in northern Idaho and eastern Washington. Since 1963, he has taught writing and cultural studies at several colleges and universities on both sides of the Pacific.

Recipient of three National Endowment for the Arts fellowships, he has also been awarded the Lingnan American Studies fellowship in Hong Kong and a Senior Fulbright lectureship in Changchun, a Rockefeller Bellagio residency, and several research awards, including one from the United Nations for on-site backgrounding for this novel. He has been appointed distinguished writer-in-residence at Fudan University, Knox College and Mercy Corps.

In 2002, his collection *Lipstick and Other Stories* received the American Book Award.